New Fantasies

by Richard R. Kennedy

Published by Author

Second printing

(© 1990, 2000, Unpublished. Revised : © 2006)

Other works:
http://lulu.com/spotlight/rrksr

ISBN: 978-0-6151-5809-9

Richard R. Kennedy, publisher
Boynton Beach, FL 33426

Printed in the United States of America

Dedicated to:

Those of all ages
who have been
fond of Traditional
Fairy Tales.

New Fantasies: Fables for All Ages

Titles

Atlantis Regained

There was a mermaid unlike any other. Mermaids are sleek long-haired beauties that like to be together, frolic and swim the seven seas. This one had a round, chubby, happy face, which too often was transfigured to sagging and sad by the cruel wagging tongues and flapping fins of her sleek cousins. These lovelies of every sailor's dream called her Walrus because of her overbite and lumpy size. They would have nothing to do with her and would not allow her to accompany them when they followed the ships, lest the maritime net her into its dreams and ruin the legend of the beauteous maidens of the sea.

Rather than be sad for the rest of her life, she decided that she was her own best friend and worked on becoming content with herself. She wanted only a secluded cove to live in and rest her fins on a lonely jetty. She scoured the Mediterranean Sea hoping to find the ancient lost city she had heard so much about from her mentor, a giant sea turtle, rumored throughout the fin world to be thousands of years old. Unfortunately so was the great turtle's memory which was fading and his directions were not clear. After years she finally gave up, thinking that the turtle obviously was imagining such a place.

She then toured the seas looking for sunken ships but all she could find were rotting hulls and furniture mangled by clumsy sharks. Then one day, a very clear day, and having crossed the great Atlantic, she found an island above with tall buildings glistening in the sunlight. At night it was even more glorious as the skyline glowed in all color of light. Oh, how she wished she could live on that island! She settled for second best and chose to live under it among its many reefs and piers. Besides, she had learned from the ancient turtle that humans could be crueler than her flapping cousins.

While she swam round the island and took in the splendid

sights, high above her on this island a tall, thin man in a mansion midst tall buildings held a meeting in his office. He stood at the end of a long gleaming table. Sitting at this table were other men all dressed in blue boring business suits just as he was.

The tall man slammed his brown fist on the shiny surface and growled, "This insult must end! For over seventy-five years we were known as the city with the tallest buildings and now these upstart cities are throwing up taller ones as if they were toy blocks and erector sets."

A gray-haired city planner who had contributed his expertise to the construction of many of the city's skyscrapers and the oldest at the table, cleared his voice in an effort to clip his leader's wings, "Mr. Mayor I warned you about this. There is nothing we can do about it. It is the law of physics. Our tiny island is over-built as it is."

"Poppycock!" stormed back the thin mayor, making it clear to the younger men that the old city planner was not to be taken seriously. "This is the greatest city in the history of man, and we shall make it even greater!" With a great flourish the mayor rolled out a large blueprint of a building. "Now, this is what I want you to start on immediately — a mile high skyscraper. I call it a space-scraper!" The younger men of the Lego generation — all gathered wide-eyed round the blueprint; then eyed each other with sparkling excitement. All of the young builders but the eldest who was caught between the rigidity of erector-sets and the flexibility of Lego, agreed it could be done and were eager to start the gargantuan project right away. They turned deaf ear to the old city planner's repeated warning that the proposed building would be too heavy.

For years — the ambitious project was nearing its one mile summit — the mermaid continued her tour of the island, never tiring of its many wonders — its bridges, the immense ships in and out of the harbor, the splendid yachts and stately sailboats parading the rivers, the millions of automobiles that crossed the bridges and sped along the edge of the island, and the brilliant lights at night that outshone even the stars. But for the endless traffic of garbage scows, she was happy with her chosen neighborhood; still, she could not overcome her cousins rejection resulting in lasting loneliness and never a night would go by that she didn't dream of living on the island rather than under it.

One evening as the sun sunk behind the skyline, she swam out to greet the large lady in the harbor. How often the pleasant, plump mermaid wished that the lady would speak to her or bend a knee and swoop her up in her immense arms! Suddenly from behind she felt a massive undercurrent. The great lady above tilted. She thought: Did the lady see her? Was she really going to take her up in her arms? But then the excited mermaid was abruptly propelled through the harbor and way out into the ocean. No matter how much she flipped her fins and paddled her arms she could not fight off the winnowing tidal wave above. She could not understand how a tidal wave could have started from the harbor.

Finally the giant force subsided into the night and she began to swim back to her home. While swimming she looked above for the beacon in the lady's hand. She could not find it: "Could I have been pushed out to sea further than I thought?" Then she looked down into the murky depths. To her surprise and delight the lady was staring *up* at her! Her great face shining from the light in her arm. "The great lady has chosen to visit me!" she bubbled. "Perhaps to live with me, knowing I could not go to her."

The mermaid in sinuous delight flipped round the lady whose lips seemed to bubble out a kiss, inspiring her to swim up to caress one of her cheeks with her chubby hands and wiggle her fins in her ear. Looking up into the lady's great eyes, the mermaid blinked her eyes, hoping the enormous ones would too. But the great lady seemed to just stare up at the stars overhead — stars the lady had never seen before. The mermaid swam up to look directly into her eyes. They twinkled with starlight and the mermaid was satisfied that the lady was looking at her warmly. She swam to sit on the book

7

edge nestled to the lady's breast. Her fat cheeks hollowed from sighing bubbles of thankfulness.

She then gazed up to take in the city lights. The mermaid wondered why they had not lit the tops of the buildings as they always do until she squinted into the night's dark waters and it seemed as though there were no buildings, no piers, no shore. She peered further north—still nothing, but below in the water she saw many lights flickering and seemingly one by one going out.

She left the lady's arm and swam further into the harbor. She flipped sinuously with joy; the entire island had sunk deeply into the harbor, whirling the lady's tiny satellite island under the surface as well. Her wish came true. She now lived *on* the island — it had come to her! Wriggling her webbed toes, she bubbled, "My, the wise old turtle was talking not of the distant past but of the future!"

Reluctant Easter Bunny

A very long time ago, the Controller of Holidays from high in the sky, summoned the mayor of Hareburg, a peaceful haven for rabbits that had retired from life on earth.

The mayor, a prize white rabbit in his term on earth, was annoyed that he was called upon in the middle of a city-wide race where the fastest rabbits and hares competed in their chase of a mechanical dog.

The Controller — on earth he had been a coordinator of Roman holidays during the decline of the empire — said with a sigh and a weary tone, "Mayor, we have a problem down below during Easter. Earthlings are never content, much like in old Rome. A new custom has sprung up known as Easter eggs — and in color no less. Some weird artist colony down there came up with the idea."

The mayor flapped an ear. "So? It's not my problem; see

Mother Hen about it," he said annoyed, bucking a tooth at the controller. "I've got to get back to the race in time to award the prize."

The controller smirked. "Oh, that can wait. I've lengthened the race and sped up the dog."

"That's a dirty trick,"the mayor clattered. "Speaking of dirty tricks, I've heard from the tree of knowledge that you, my high and mighty controller, in some decade or century, plan to initiate sporty humans into breeding dogs for chasing a mechanical rabbit."

The Controller flapped his beard — he gave up on the clean shaven Roman style, which he always hated. "Well, I've always been a dog lover…anyway, thank the Lord it's mechanical and not the real thing. For if I had total jurisdiction…"

"Never mind. You don't have control over my town — you'd have lions after us like we were Christians.…By the way, how did you ever get up here, anyway?"

With the wave of a hand, the most high bureaucrat, said, "Forgiveness, you know.…Enough of this chatter," while thumbing through papers. "We've got to come up with a way to deliver the eggs," the controller added, tossing his long white beard to the soft breeze in the sky.

"Oh, is that all? — Why, that's easy! You're such a dog lover I'm surprised you didn't think of it," the bunny mayor said nonchalantly.

"What's a dog got to do with eggs?" the controller asked, looking confused.

"Uh, yes,…I might ask what has a bunny to do with it, too," said the mayor. "But the point is there are many dogs known for their working ability — just ask the Eskimos. Whoever heard of a work rabbit and an artist to boot?"

"I heard you do wonderfully when you stick those long ears in paint.… Still, you can't expect an Eskimo dog to work in spring climate," the Controller shot back.

9

"Perhaps not, but surely a Saint Bernard is qualified for a delivery job in any season — well, maybe he'll need a haircut — and he can stick his tail in paint." The mayor stood up an ear and added, "Well, that's settled…back to the races." The mayor turned to go.

The controller reached out, holding the mayor in check by the ear. "Not so fast — even though rabbits are supposed to be quick."

"Apparently not as quick as you, old man," the mayor was quick to reply. "Not bad for one well into his second millennium…. So, you don't like my idea — leaving it to the dogs, eh?"

The controller's long beard trailed the shake of his head." You forget I favor dogs," the controller said. "Why on earth would I want to send one on such a silly task as delivering eggs!"

"Good, then let's forget it altogether. Indeed, scramble the egg idea, let them — those silly humans — get Jack to deliver beans — and his friendly giant can shaped them to look like eggs."

"They already do that down there, and that's where they got the idea from!"

The mayors ears stood up straight. "How can you get eggs from beans?"

"I don't know but they did. The jelly beans are not beans at all, but jelly eggs!" The Controller shook his head in bewilderment.

"Good grief, that's silly!" cried the bunny.

"But the humans do have a point," the comptroller said, shaking his head.

"Yeah, pointed heads! Those humans don't deserve the holiday — you ought to cancel it altogether — if not, at least tell them to cut out the egg nonsense!" the mayor bellyached.

"See? That's why you're a rabbit — you'll never be an egghead. Don't you get it? The egg idea is the celebration of new life," the controller instructed the poor befuddled mayor.

"Well, I still have ears. And I tell you I heard the best representation of life is babies. So call on the stork and leave me to my races."

"No, that won't do — we need the seed," the Controller said stubbornly.

Just as stubbornly the mayor replied, "Then call up Johnny Appleseed — apples make about as much sense as eggs!"

"I'm afraid it has been all settled by a higher authority. Eggs it must be," the Controller said grimly.

"Oh, I get it. That new guy that was elected to the board, eh? — the one from the Dairy Association! Then have your eggs, in spite of the cholesterol — uh, gee, they don't know about LDL and stuff yet — anyway, do what you must but leave us rabbits out of this clucky idea," the mayor urged.

"I guess you're not as stupid as I thought," the comptroller said in a surprised tone. "That's precisely why Mother Hen refuses the job. Aside from constantly having to abort her life-giving ways, she's afraid that if chickens deliver the eggs humans will come up with the idea that eggs are loaded with it, but poultry has less cholesterol, and more and more, chickens will be the staple diet of humans. Your kind has nothing to worry about...since you're so greasy...."

"Enough, you win — for the sake of the chicken flock. Now, please let me get back to the races." He turned and sped off, but then stopped short and turned back. "Are you sure you won't reconsider Jack and the Beanstalk or the Saint Bernard?"

The controller shook his head and, with his beard waved away the frustrated mayor, answering, "Not even Saint Nick."

Nellie And The Crows

The farmer Nice called, "Here, Nellie," to his only cow, which was grazing in the pasture. "Come get your supper." The cow came loping in but quicker than usual toward a wire fence as Mr. Nice tossed over to her the cobs of freshly eaten corn.

11

Nellie loved this time of year when the Nice family feasted on fresh corn-on-the-cob. It tasted so much sweeter than the dried out winter corn the farmer ground up for her. The farmer's children especially left her many tasty kernels on their cobs along with the delicious saturation of her very own milk the farmer had made into butter.

Crows, too, liked corn, especially the human leftover kind at Nellie's supper hour. She could not really enjoy her supper because crows would swoop in on her and fight for the golden kernels. As much as she would moo, shake her horns, whip her tail and raise her hoofs, the feisty birds would just fly off for a moment and then zoom back to snatch more prize buttery kernels.

This same evening Nellie was in for another treat because the youngest son, Allie, came out with another platter of corn — many of them not even eaten. Allie threw stones at the giant black birds to scatter them and then gently flipped the cobs through the fence.

As he very carefully slid the last full cob through the fence, he said, "There, Nellie,...almost like a Thanksgiving dinner. I put a fat glob of your special butter on it." Nellie wiggled her ears and brushed her bony cheek along the little boy's arm. Allie patted her horns and turned to walk away, but reeled back when she mooed that the crows had returned to steal her corn. He understood and climbed the fence to chase the aggressive wingers away; but as soon as little Allie climbed back over, they would fly back to their thieving ways, despite Nellie's protesting moos and contortions.

Little Allie became angry and headed for the barn. He returned with his cap pistol and fired a full roll into the air. The crows scattered, but so did Nellie, who was frightened by the repeating, cracking sound. Allie put the cap pistol back in his pocket and coaxed her back to her supper. Her worried brown eyes dissolved by his touch and comforting voice, and she continued her feast.

The crows were startled only for a moment by the noisy caps and swooped back to their loot as soon as the boy sat under a tree nearby. Growling and shouting, the lad waved his arms threateningly as he darted toward them. The experienced crows, knowing the little boy never carried one — he was forbidden to use it — feared only farmer Nice's booming shotgun in the cornfields. They boldly winged their assault on the corn at strategic intervals.

The next evening, after Allie had begged his father half the day, Nellie was called in from the pasture for a heaping platter of corn. Allie held a full ear of the prize corn for her. Though she was a little restive, Nellie trusted the boy completely while he fussed round her wiggling ears.

The crows circled round cawing, perhaps confused and cautious; then the largest of the flock boldly swooped down, yet keeping its distance. Suddenly a series of deafening explosions filled the evening air. Drained of its daring, the giant leader croaked hideously and flew high and away and the flock followed with nervous wings as though a hawk were attacking. Nellie just calmly continued feasting on her tempting supper.

Undisturbed by the scavenging crows and perhaps harassed never again, Nellie licked off her very own butter before biting into the succulent cobs. Peacefully, Nellie feasted next to a duplicate scarecrow from the field dressed in the farmer's straw hat and old clothing. Tied to the sleeved crossbar was — not a wooden one like in the field — farmer Nice's real shotgun, though unloaded, raised to the sky's setting sun.

Behind the tree was Allie, softly giggling but hoping the crows would once more try their luck. He still had some mighty powerful firecrackers left over from the Fourth to set off, knowing Nellie wouldn't mind — now that her ears were stuffed with cotton.

Country Boy

Not too long ago, about the time today's grandparents were children, a country boy of about thirteen after raking out farmer

13

Swenson's barnyard, had just finished neatly laying fresh hay across the extensive pen. He retired to the barn and hung up the shovel, hook and rake. Mr. Swenson popped out from a stall, having unharnessed his hitch horse. He approached the boy and took out a worn-down fifty cent piece. "My cows won't know the yard when I bring'm in from the pasture after supper," the old, tired farmer said. "You did a fine job, Del."

The half dollar tingled in the boy's hand, rushing a feeling of pride to the heart. His eyes danced with gratitude: he was expecting only thirty-five cents, "Gee, thanks, Mr. Swenson," the boy yelped and squeezed the warm coin.

The farmer removed his straw hat momentarily to wipe his pale forehead with his sleeve, then said regretfully, "Only wish we could help you out more." Sucking in tawny, hollow cheeks, smacking thin lips, he shook his agéd head and bemoaned, "But the miss's says she's got plenty of quilts...what with all the kids gone....Now, you will explain that to May,...your mom, won't you?" He tapped the boy's bony shoulder. "You're welcome to stay for eats."

"I wish I could but gotta get home, you know." The boy's stomach growled.

"Yep, I know,...what with poor May being alone now." The farmer's eyes cast downward. He tapped the boy's shoulder again and left.

Before running through Swenson's cornfield on the way home, the boy, whom his father had nick-named Del after FDR was elected for the first time, wrapped his proud half dollar in his red and white and kerchief and stuffed it into his coverall pocket. Then carefully he picked up by its coarse twine a large fluffy package wrapped in brown paper. He was disappointed that he had to take the quilt back home with him.

Bolting out of Swenson's cornfield, squeezing the package under his arm, he jumped a fence and headed for a dirt road twisting toward home. There was a stream nearby; and anxious or not Del wished he had brought his fishing pole with him so he could catch a fish for supper. Del knew that about now his mother would be busy at the stove preparing grits and scrambled eggs. Since his father no longer worked the farm, having contracted tuberculosis and sent off to a sanitarium, the family was "without, by the bye," his mother would couch, dreading the word "poor." How happy Mom would be when she saw the liberty lady on his well-earned coin this day! Now she could add it to her egg money and have enough to buy from the general store the thread and filler material she needed to complete a quilt for an old widow, who was giving her five dollars for his mother's handiwork. But she would not be happy that Swenson did not buy the quilt Del squeezed under his arm. Because the old widow ordered one with very different colors, his mother could not just sell this one to her. Besides, even if the widow did want this one, she would have to settle for only four dollars on one not made to order.

As he crossed an old wooden bridge spanning the stream he always fished, he looked below at a wooded section beyond the bank. The expected mixture of pride and disappointment in his mother face came to mind, and he wished it could boast a beaming smile always. He took his familiar path from the bridge to the wooded section. Brushing away some underbrush he picked up an old pie pan with holes in the bottom, went to the stream's bed, perched on a rock and started to pan for the gold in his imagination bonded to putting a smile on his mother's face. Two years ago when in town with his father he had heard some men in front of the general store jokingly talking about an old prospector who had panned for gold in the stream nearly a century ago, and had sifted a small mountain of fool's gold. Nevertheless, the boy would try the pan whenever he tired of fishing, or the big pesky fish he was after kept getting away from him. His father told him that the fish, because of its gold streaks, apparently was to be a prize-bred goldfish but refused to color and was returned to its wild carp state.

15

His father swore the johnny carp had gathered up some intelligence from human captivity, "if you can believe old fisherman tales." Screening with the pan for several minutes, Del caught in the corner of his eye, the gold jaw protrude the surface in the middle of the stream. He wished again that he had his pole. He noted that next time he would hide it away with his pan.

In a tattered straw hat, whitish-gray locks peeping from the pate and stringy gray hair extending in disarray from the brim, a little old lady crossed the bridge pushing with nary a grunt or huff — belying her size and age — a peddler's cart. Seeing him she stopped the cart and yelled down, chuckling, "This stream's a long way from the Klondike, sonny,...no gold in these parts."

The boy looked up squinting into the drooping sun peeping through trees. "Maybe, but I don't give up hoping."

She cackled, "That's not hoping, my boy, that's dreaming. But, heck, what's a boy without his dreams, eh?" And she chuckled again, then asked, "Sonny, how far to the Swenson farm?"

"Not far," he said, "just around the bend and beyond a cornfield. "Ah, yes, I heard he grows real fine corn," she said, leaning against the bridge railing.

"Oh, yeah, the best, but it'll need another couple of weeks," he rejoined, continuing with his panning as he did not wish to chat. He knew old people loved to waste time talking.

"Too bad, I could've worked a trade. But on the route back I should be just right for the pickin's," she said mildly disappointed while reaching into a small satchel slinging from her shoulder and pulled out a corncob pipe. She poured tobacco into it mechanically and struck a wooden match. After several puffs she said, waving a veiny, skinny hand to cut the smoke, "Seldom been in these parts before....Don't know as I will ever make a habit of it. People don't seem to have any money. I mean a lot less than most."

"Yeah? You been here before? Ain't never seen ya....Yep, hard times, ma'am. We've been selling our eggs for less than twenty-five cents lately — last year we got thirty," he said, getting up from his knees and turning to nestle the pan back in the underbrush. He picked up his package and started back up the path.

When he did not head back for the bridge, she crowed, "Say, lad, what's your hurry? Don't tell me you found gold."

He jerked his head around, chuckled and answered, "Oh, I gotta get home. And I suppose it *is* just a dream."

"Still, don't give up on it — keeps you young. . . . Didn't look like you were hankering to get home when you were playing with that mining pan. . . I have many fine trinkets and toys in my cart — these aren't just dreams, but the real thing. Wouldn't you like to look 'em over?"

He looked back over his shoulder and said, "No thank you. I must get home for supper." But he glanced a second time, spotting a fishing pole resting against the cart sideboard. He stopped and edged back a few steps and paused before the cart, ignoring the hundreds of wares except the rod.

"Something here caught your eye, eh?" she said with a toothless smile.

"Gee, that's a good-looking fishing rod you have there," he said. "The very best and it comes with a very special lure and line," she said, taking it out of the cart bracket.

"Oh, don't bother to show me," he jumped. "I really have to go — besides I have no money and it looks like it has zillions of dollar signs all over it."

The woman chuckled and coughed on her smoke. "You have a good eye, lad. The best is always expensive, but not out of reach." She winked and raised a gray, unruly brow. "Why, with this rod you can catch more fish than if you used a fisherman's net."

His eyes brightened. "Really?"

"Yep,. . .of course, what does a country boy know about investing," she said as she mimicked casting with the rod, while sucking on the pipe.

17

"Oh, a little...but it does no good to know something if you can't use it. My father always says you got to have money to make money. And like I say, I ain't got it."

She shook her head. "Customers always say they don't have money until they want or need something, then all of sudden they come up with it." She put the rod back in its slot. "You know, lad, spending is sometimes as big a sacrifice as saving."

He grinned. "I guess folks here don't need to worry none about neither, then, 'cause a lot of folks in these parts fell into hard times, ma'am. I suspect that's why your cart's still full and here it's practically the end of the day. You said yourself you might not be back."

She showed a toothless grin again and cackled, "Well, maybe, maybe not. But this ain't no vegetable cart— got a week's work in this old wagon....Smart lad, though, you see things pretty good...except seeing can be deceiving."

"What do you mean? I always thought seeing is believing," he said, staring at the rod standing proud in its bracket.

"Well, take this fishing rod, for instance," she added, taking it down from the cart again and swinging it in front of him. "This is no ordinary fishing rod."

"Well, it's sure nice looking, and I'm sure it casts nice; but I doubt it could do much more than my ordinary birch pole."

"Well, now, sonny, that's where you're wrong. You said before you have to have money to make money — maybe so — but you also got to have the tools too," she said.

"Yeah, I know that," he said confidently, putting down the package. "You see," he took out his red and white handkerchief. "In here I have fifty cents. I earned it using farmer Swenson's rake and shovel. Yep, just two common tools made that for me. But, anyhow, my mother can turn that half dollar into five whole dollars in a few days. That's what you mean by investing, right?"

"My, you *are* a smart lad. That's some handsome investment —

except what's five dollars when you can make hundreds with this fishing rod."

"Shucks, ma'am," he uttered, flashing his eyes over the bridge railing and smiling, "you're pulling my leg....Ain't that much fish in this stream to make that kind of money!"

She guffawed, then said, "Just like I said, you're a right smart lad. But who says there's no fish? Besides one super catch makes all the difference, eh? This special lure will do wonders." She held up golden fly wings.

"Looks like a butterfly. Pretty but what's so special about it if it can only draw one fish?" he asked, although he was lured by the lure.

"I didn't say that, laddy. Why, you won't know it's the same stream once you get started."

He rubbed his chin. "I sure wouldn't mind one fish tonight for supper, though."

"Then, my boy, with that fifty-cent piece, you can borrow it for fifteen minutes," she said anxiously. "Even got the bait."

He shook his head, picked up his package and said,"Not even worth a quarter just to borrow it for one fish — heck, a half a buck'd buy three pounds at the market....Any how, I couldn't give up my money — told ya my mom needs it."

"Then I'll give you a quarter change. A quarter doesn't go very far these days — not for me." She touched her aquiline nose. "Yet on the other hand it does — for you. Think of all the ice-cream and candy you'll get from the change," she said looking intently at his fluffy package. "What else does a boy your age need money for?"

"Jeepers, I already told ya what for — but that's right for sure, a quarter ain't much, unless you can spend it on treats, then it goes a long way. But money's too important to waste on baby junk. Our hens have to lay a dozen for us to get near a quarter and it costs us about ten cents to feed them for every dozen they lay."

"Oh, yes, the good Lord provides but not without your sweat,"

19

she cackled. "You got a clear head on your shoulders, sonny; you're darn near a grown up….Say, what's in the package? — looks like a pillow."

"It's a quilt. My mom was hoping Mrs. Swenson would buy it; but she said she'd probably wait till winter."

"That would make sense, excepting' it gets mighty cold around here at night — of course, your young blood wouldn't feel it," she said as she rubbed her back.

"Gee, maybe you'd like to buy it!" he said excitedly.

"No, sonny,…got plenty on my bed." She pointed to a roll of blankets on the cart. "But I'd like to see it…to tell what kind of work your mother does."

"Oh, she's good, all right," he said proudly. "Trouble is most people round here are too poor to buy my mom's fine needlework."

"That good, eh? Well, let's see." He unwrapped it. The quilt puffed up as though eager to show off its splendid colors. "My, my, your mother really is talented. I must meet her on my way back. I think I could sell them in town — not without a lot of sweat, mind you."

"Really? I mean, you really think so? With my dad being sick and all, it sure would be a big help." Then he eyed her skeptically. "Aw, shucks, you can't even sell what's in your cart."

"Oh, don't fret none about me, sonny; I do okay. Still, I have to be sure in my business….I tell you what. I'll trade the rod for the quilt. And if the quilt sells — and I don't see why it won't — I'll come back and make a tempty deal with your mother to buy more."

At first he jumped with joy until he thought about it. "No, I couldn't, my ma would kill me. My old pole is just as good."

"You won't think that once you try this fine instrument. I tell you it will make more for you than a hundred quilts."

"Aw, shucks, ma'am, you're like the devil trying to tempt me and gettin' me in trouble," he said while she turned to take the rod out of its bracket.

20

She laughed. "A kind old lady like me? — the devil! — no, laddy, I just want to help, what with your father sick."

"Jeez, I don't know, my ma would be awful upset with me. Why, she'd say the same thing as I'm thinking: that I got a fishing pole already," he pined, scratching his dark hair grown bushy over the summer.

"You ain't got a real fishing rod — and what's more not like this spectacular one." She whipped it before his admiring eyes. She held it out for him.

"No question there," he said as he gripped its wonderful warm corked handle.

"You say your mom would be upset, but how's she going to feel when you return with that fine quilt unsold?" she prodded.

He shrugged and asked, "What makes you think I can catch more fish than I do now?"

"Ah, my boy, that's the beauty of a prize, new possession. Why, it's the same as a farmer who farms better with a new tractor. It performs better and he just feels a whole lot better....You'll feel better, too."

"But I want the fishing to be better. I don't just want to feel good."

"Don't fret; look at this tackle — how can you not be better at it? Why, on the coast you could catch sharks with that fine rod," she smiled, though tight lipped.

He chuckled. "I'd be happy with the one big fish down there that likes driving me crazy. I swear it grows bigger every year — why, it's darn near two feet now!" He gestured with the rod toward the stream underneath before reluctantly handing it back to her.

"There you are, then, sonny....You got your fish with this little treasure here," she squeaked with confidence as she touched the rod and then thrust it back to him. "Tell you what. If you don't catch that fish by the end of the summer. I'll pay you for the quilt and you can keep the rod."

21

His eyes brightened. "Yeah?...You mean it?...Aw, shucks, how do I know?...I never saw you round these parts before and like as I'll never see you again."

She laughed and clacked, "My, for a young lad you sure do worry a lot! Why, at your age I didn't have a care in the world."

"Well, maybe there were better times then," fell from his lips quite unconsciously, so involved was he in snapping the gleaming rod that seemed magical in the setting sun.

Chuckling and showing her toothless grin, she said, "Oh, all generations have their ups and downs. And you'll be on the upswing, sonny — guaranteed — with this tackle."

"Jeez, ma'am, you really think so?...I mean, you wouldn't cheat me, would you?" He searched her weather-beaten face.

"Cheat you?...Why, my boy, I'm cheating myself!"she said with an annoyed undertone. "Here I am a business woman — all my life I've scraped a living out of bartering and selling — and I'm offering you a fine rod for a quilt you can't even sell." She grasped the rod from him and turned to put it back in the cart. "That's the thanks I get for wanting to make a selfish little boy happy."

"Jeez, ma'am, don't get loony. I'm sorry, really, I mean, I really do think it's a good deal....It's just that...well, my mother,..."

"Think of it as *for* your mother, lad, that you want it." she said turning toward him. "I tell you, if you have faith in yourself, things have a way of working for you."

"But you just corked off I was selfish."

"No, I didn't mean it that way. I wouldn't still be here talking to you if I saw that in you. It's that you want to have cornbread and butter it too. The world doesn't work that way, laddy. Oh, I could just give you this fine tool for the half dollar in your pocket and come back every two weeks for a quarter at a time, chancing you had it. But that's not going to teach you the ways of the world. Didn't you say times are hard? So why would you expect it to be easy now? — and yet make it hard for me. Do you see, boy — get what I'm saying? — maybe you don't have the grit for this world."

He was almost in tears, and he quickly thrust the quilt in her arms. "I do too have the grit! I'll show you!" He reached up and grabbed the rod, then looked into her eyes for the first time. They were a crystal hazel and looked so young, not the yellowing eyes of age he had so often observed in old people. "That is, if you let me," he pleaded.

Her eyes sparkled incongruently with her toothless smile. "That's the old spirit, sonny. Go out and hook the world!"

Several weeks later the old woman boldly knocked on the door of the boy's house. The mother, rather tall, bent and thin, had seen the peddler, fitting Dell's description, from the window coming up the road. She answered the door. Looking at the old woman coldly, she said, "Well, now, you certainly have nerve coming here after coaxing the quilt from my son!"

The old woman chuckled with tight lips and her warm eyes crossed the mother's tired ones. "Oh, you can't barter without nerve, sweet lady. Least of all kindness, which I showed plenty of in dealing with your nice boy."

The mother's soft eyes managed to stir up a storm. "Surely, you know it was not his business to barter away the quilt. Common decency would have been for you to deal with me,"

"True, truly said; still, I know the boy wanted that fishing rod and if I had seen you, I suspect you'd flat-out refuse."

"Oh, thinking of the wishes of my son, is that it?...Sure, none of your business. And to fill my son with a luxury such as that under the circumstances is like stealing milk from a nursing cow," she said, her eyes still stormy.

"Oh, now, if that's what you really think, I'll gladly take it back," she said confidently.

May vented her vexation by scowling and folding her arms. "Oh, I'm sure you would — in a pig's eye. And what about my five dollar quilt?"

23

"Well, now, that's why I'm here. I sold it and would like to buy some more from you. But I have to tell you: you ain't got a head for business if you think they're worth that much. Why, I had to go clear into the second town from here to get just four dollars — the fishing rod cost me three times that! People aren't thinking quilts in the summer, you know."

"Strange the widow down the road from here ordered one and paid me seven-fifty." Del's mother said, biting her lip over the lie.

"Ordered? Oh, well, and finely made to her specifications, no doubt. That I would believe. But that isn't the normal market, sweet lady — and certain it's not here in these parts.... Why, most folks round here patch up their own. Granted not with your fine needlework, but they keep warm."

"Like my son's old fishing pole served the same purpose as his new, fancy one, eh?" May said; her now softening eyes peering under the old woman's hat.

"Oh? And how is he doing? Caught plenty I'll wager."

"Then you'd lose. Nothing spectacular — certainly no more, perhaps less, than with his old homemade pole," May in response lashed back, but in reality she had gotten over it.

"Oh, well, takes a while to get used to, I guess. But the difference between a bad fisherman and a good one is in the amount of patience, you know."

"And that I have too," May lied. "That's why I feel I can sell my quilts for at least five dollars."

"Suit yourself, then, ma'am. But I think you're making a big mistake. I stopped at practically every home round here, and not one of them was interested in your quilt. I carried it around for two weeks and twenty-five miles from here before I could get three dollars."

"Why, that's ridiculous! It costs me one-fifty in materials!— not to mention the hours involved. Besides, you said four before."

"Uh,...after my costs. Yes, the sad truth is that labor is cheap in these times," the old woman mused. "Now, I'll admit you make a fine quilt and they are worth a lot more. But you would have to travel into the big city to get that kind of money — maybe even seven-fifty. Are you willing to spend three weeks away from home and a hundred miles from here to get your price?"

"No, I suppose not...but perhaps you could."

She laughed. "Not at my age, sweet lady. I go only as far as my cart and legs will take me."

The mother warmed up a little toward her and laughed. There was something about the old woman she liked. Perhaps it was her pluck that dragged herself round the country-side all alone. Yes, it was her independence — an old veteran of self-reliance. May, on the other hand, was just a novice, what with her husband in the sanitarium less than a month. "Of course, it was unkind of me, considering your age, to suggest such a thing....I'm not myself.... Actually, I'm glad you traded with my son. It made him very happy. We can't give him anything but ourselves. So in a strange way you did us a favor."

"Well, I see now that you are a stranger to unkindness....I tell you what....I'll give you three and a half dollars for each quilt. If I'm lucky in the next town and can get better than seven, we'll split the amount over that."

"That isn't very generous. Why, if you sell them for seven dollars you keep it all and make as much as me without the costs."

"Oh, but I do have costs, sweet lady. I'm always on the road — can't settle into a fine home like you have. It costs money for meals and board, you know."

"Yes, I suppose that's true." Then she reflected. "But, say, you just don't sell quilts — why, you're like those newfangled supermarkets!" Craning her neck she added, "Look at all the tools and wares you have in the cart. I even see another fishing rod — must bring a handsome profit or you wouldn't be carrying another around."

25

The peddler shook her head vigorously and refuted her, "No, good lady, that rod there could never compare to the one your son has."

Dell's mother smirked and went on, "And as far as room and board go, people say they see you sleeping in your cart and farmers are complaining that you steal their vegetables to boil

"Really, the few times I've been in these parts and already I have a reputation—that could be good for business." She laughed. "Leastwise that doesn't make me a chicken thief. What's a few ears of corn or a handful of beans and peas in these large lush fields. Nor do I ever go beggin'. Still, I can't very well sleep out in the rain or in the winter, so I do have expenses, especially in the towns."

"Well, how do I know you will try to get more than seven dollars when you have to split with me? I mean, isn't it easier to settle for less than to negotiate for more?"

"Well, to be honest, it depends on the market. Here in the summer I doubt that will happen. But in the fall and winter the price is bound to go up. Besides if I have a chance to make fifty more cents on a dollar I'll work at it, rest assure."

"Hmm, I see now why my son came home minus a quilt that day."

"No, ma'am, it's just the way things are. You can't help yourself. But I can help you. It does no good to make quilts if you can't sell them. There always has to be a market for a commodity. Like your boy was telling me about the falling price of eggs."

"Oh, my, yes,. . . down to eighteen cents." She looked into the old woman's eyes. She was hoping for a miracle in light of the pride she took in her needlework. But the truth was that she was not getting anywhere. Just as the woman said. Almost everyone made her own. Simple folk who just wanted warmth in their beds. They didn't care how the patch quilts looked. She was ashamed that she lied about the widow, who had actually reneged and canceled the order. Since the boy came home with the fishing rod she had made three more quilts plus the widow's. She motioned for the woman to step into the modest room and quickly served her a glass of iced-tea. She then went over to a sewing machine on whose work space was piled the four quilts.

Though she had seen factory-made quilts for as much as twelve dollars for extra-large ones in the general store, not many bought them at that price. Desperate, she handed them to the woman. She tried to hide her glee when the old woman peeled off fourteen dollar bills from their fat parent roll. Del's mother felt wealthy: if only for a brief moment it lifted her spirits. She understood how her boy must have felt. The two women shook hands. "Well, now that we are partners of sorts,...my name is May...and yours?"

"Oh, my, no one in my route has ever asked before." The old woman chuckled. "Back in the city where I get my supplies they call me Myrna."

"Really! My,...an unusual name...Like Myrna Loy!" "Hah, that's funny!" Myrna's eyes twinkled. "Never accuse us of being two peas in a pod, eh?" They both laughed over the conceit of juxtaposition.

Del continued through the summer to fish by the stream — more often than normally — but with little luck. Though the new rod did little, he was so enthralled by it that he never once tired and turn to his pan of dreams; and, of course, it was a great sense of satisfaction to him that he could cast further and with greater ease; yet ironically it added to the frustration because he was preoccupied with the carp that seemed to be mocking him by quivering sinuously near the shore as though showing off its growing size and golden streaks, daring him more as though it knew the boy above had a new rod. It became so frustrating to him that it seemed the hook was out of the water more than it was in, so frequently did he cast directly toward the pesky johnny. Adding to this was that the summer was winding down and there was less than a week before he would be back in school. What with his chores and school that would steal his time from the stream, he was almost at wit's end.

One day the old peddler crossed the bridge on her way back from his home. He looked up at the cart and saw his mother's quilts. He called to her, "Gettin' near school time and I still haven't caught the big one. Remember what you said."

She guffawed and yelled back. "Just sales talk, young man. Still haven't learned the ways of the world. Well, you got time — the summer's not over — have faith." She touched the brim of her hat and pushed on.

Each time the old woman had return to the boy's home, the mother had several more quilts for her to sell. The tall, drawn woman — her bowed stature seemed more straightened now — was becoming almost giddy that she was finally generating some income. When the old woman returned on the second visit she handed May an additional two dollars.

"You were right, May, I was able to sell them for eight dollars!" she said with a flourish. "I guess, their old bones are beginning to feel winter in the air."

"Oh, thanks to the Lord — and you, dear Myrna! Bring on an early winter." The mother said merrily.

On the third visit the old woman handed her an additional three dollars for having sold four quilts at $8.50. "Oh, my," cried the mother, "and just the other day eggs went back up to twenty-two cents! Oh, good woman, you are truly God-sent! You are worth every penny of your outrageous profits!" And they both laughed convulsively.

The fourth visit— just before school was to open — the old woman greeted the woman with a sad look and said, "You were so joyous the last time, that I hate to disappoint you. So even though I couldn't sell them for as much, I'm going to give you the entire amount above the seven. That makes one dollar more for each of the five that I sold for only eight."

The mother squealed with joy and hugged the old woman. But then said solemnly, "Oh, my dear, you work so hard. I just couldn't.

I've said such cruel things…"

"Don't fret about it. People pipe off all the time about us sales-people. After all, what do we do? We can't make anything. Take your boy, you bring him up right in teaching him the value of labor. He not only sells eggs — I could do that — but he cares for and feeds the chickens that lay them. And the feed you grow to boot. And the fishing rod…I can only present it, he has to catch the fish. By the way, how is he doing?"

"Oh, he's happy with it. Just doesn't catch much. Still, enough to cut down on the slaughtering of our hogs."

"There, you see?"

"Just the same….you must forgive me for the last time when I said your profits were outrageous."

Outrageous, indeed — for the old woman had not sold a single quilt for less than twelve dollars! The fine needlework was instantly recognized by customers in the far-off town. So easy did the old woman sell the quilts that she was determined that before the Christmas rush — certain she could get eighteen — she would buy a train ticket, and have the packages of quilts sent to a rickety rooming house she stayed in when she went to the big city twice a year to do her purchasing. It was the very same rooming house where her long time peddler-competitor died and left her his trinkets and wares, including the marvelous fishing rod, which he would never sell.

On Labor Day—the day before the schoolhouse bell would ring — Del spent the entire afternoon trying to catch the big carp. In spite of himself, he caught a dozen or so minnows and sunfish; the most he had ever caught in a day. He was convinced that his efficiency was gaining in his handling of the rod. He was sure that his mother now would forgive him. Though she had chastised him mercilessly at the outset, she never spoke of it again. Yet he felt she had never actually forgiven him, though mercifully she had forgotten, especially when she was doing so well with her venture

29

with the old woman.

Suddenly he felt a strong tug on the line. The rod bent full, and he deftly let out more line. Then the johnny leaped into the setting sun; its gold streaks shone. Del's heart pounded; he had never seen it breach before. The rod snapped back; the tension was gone. He reeled in an empty hook. Out of rage he hurled the rod across almost to the other side. His body ran cold when he realized what he had done. Quickly he got out of the water to get his old pole, lying in oblivion beside the pan. He waded back in to cross the stream. He extended the old pole and hooked the handle of the rod. He sighed in relief that God had forgiven him for his stupidity. Then the rod handle no longer would rise and he almost lost it from a sudden jerk against the old pole's hook. He dived in after it and grabbed the rod handle, scrambling to his feet. There in all its glory was the big fish wriggling and leaping from the imbedded hook. He back pedaled across the stream and gently reeled in the long awaited catch. He blinked his eyes several times in disbelief that the fish lay still. He was sure it would squirm resistance on its way to the pail. He was disappointed; it lay already dead — not a flap out of fin nor gill. He laid the big johnny over the others in the pail and rushed home to get out of his drenched clothes. Several times on the way, he stopped to look at the johnny. Del felt he had lost a friend.

When Del's mother went out to the chopping block where he was about to clean the fish, she spread a big smile upon seeing his splendid catches. She nudged him away from the block, urging him jubilantly, "Get out of those wet clothes and get dressed for supper. I'll clean the big one and we'll celebrate with a real meal for a change."

"I did that good, huh, Ma?" He was already celebrating her smiling face.

"Yes, indeedy," she said excitedly, "good for several suppers! And now that eggs are up to twenty-six cents, and the old peddler can't get enough of my quilts life is good to us. I feel it in my bones that your father is going to be okay soon!" She took the knife from his hand and said, "You were right in what you did, my son, in more ways than one — why, I really feel it was meant to be."

Elated, he ran into the house to clean up for supper. Minutes later he heard his mother scream. He yanked his dripping face out of the wash basin, jumped back into his wet coveralls and ran from the tiny wash room. His mother just entered the house, cradling the johnny split open in newspaper. She spread out the newspaper on the kitchen table and smiled broadly. He looked down at a strange yellow stain. Imbedded in the arches of gill filaments were some dozen little gold nuggets.

The Eighth Dwarf

All readers young and old know of the seven little men who cared for the fair princess, Snow White. Originally, however, there were eight little men. Sometime before the little men employed the princess as their housekeeper, they were busy in their mine. When not chipping away for diamonds, they would pick away for gold, then toss crude nuggets in a wagon that they nudged along a rail as they cheerfully worked. Near the end of the day they would screen them and wash away the impurities. Then they would drop the clean nuggets into a piping hot cauldron. After the melting they poured the hot liquid gold into round molds. When they cooled they had shiny, non-minted coins. Then they would put the glowing wafers in a sack. Each evening after supper they would equally divide — as they did with diamonds — the shiny pieces of the day's labor.

31

At dusk on the way from the mine to their forest home, the chubby leader of the dwarfs, carrying the bag of gold, turned around and observed that the last, and littlest, man on the line was not keeping up with the rest. The leader, oldest and fattest, gateway to the line of little pudgy men and waited for the eighth one, and he was holding them to keep them from banging against his little bony thighs. Suddenly one of the pockets tore and a gold piece fell out. The leader bent over to pick it up, then stood upright, stomach in as much as could be expected. The leader of the dwarfs scowled and shook his head, thrusting out his palm. The eighth dwarf sheepishly emptied his pockets and deposited them in the common sack.

That evening, though saddened by the episode, they voted to discharge the youngest member from their group that had always taken pride in its sense of honor and integrity. The eighth dwarf begged their forgiveness, promising never again to be dishonest. Three did weaken—after all, they reasoned he had never hoarded any diamonds from their other mine — and because he was so young, they wanted to give him another chance. Four, including the leader, held fast and the majority ruled. The minority insisted that he be given the largest and brightest golden piece from their storage room for his years of labor. Thus, the poor eighth little man was banished from his happy home and job.

With his shiny disk, together with only a dim lantern and his pick-axe of trade, went he tearfully into the darkness of the forest. While he was following a winding path, which gradually narrowed by increasing undergrowth, the forest thicket whipped and stung his face and tore his cloak until he could continue no further. He held high his lantern and found a tall tree with a large low branch. He put down his lantern and with a full swing of the pick-axe, he stuck it into the trunk of the tree. Reaching up he hung the lantern on the end of the pick and then hoisted himself up by the axe handle. He stretched for the branch and swung like a monkey onto a perch

32

whereupon he yawned, made himself comfortable along the fat limb and took out his large gold piece to admire. The moon had peeped over the kingdom's seven mountains and its silvery light cast a glow upon the glorious, faceless coin. The little man raised his bushy brows when in the coin's bright reflection he saw wandering in the woods a lovely girl with skin as white as snow—even under moonlight. She seemed frightened. The image faded; he scratched his head through his sock-like hat and put his magic coin back in his pocket. He yawned, stretched, nestled in the curve of the branch and fell asleep.

As the eighth dwarf slept into the night, the fair princess, had climbed the seven mountains half the night after having been freed by the woodsman who had not the heart to kill the lovely little princess as the wicked queen had ordered. The princess, who had always been protected and cared for by guards and servants all her life, was frightened by this strange and lonely woods as she descended the foothills. Her fears she swallowed and her heart jumped with hope when through the thicket she saw a dim light in the distance. She was sure that it was a candlelight from a window of the little house the woodsman had spoken of. As she drew nearer, though, she saw that it was a lantern hanging from a tree. Still some hundreds of paces away, she crouched under a bush when she heard wolves howling. She dared not head for the lantern. Then the moon's reflection bounced off the foothill revealing the mouth of a cave only a few steps from the bush. Silently and fearfully she crawled to the cave and went inside. She sighed in relief. Exhausted, she lay down. In a little while the beat of her lonely heart soon made her drowsy and she finally fell into a deep sleep.

Dawn cracked through the deep shadows of the forest and the birds began to chirp, welcoming the new day. The princess stirred and rolled on her back. Her eye lids parted and she blinked. A great brown bear looked down at her curiously. She screamed, rolled away and jumped to her feet. Quickly she ran out of the cave. Remembering the lantern on the tree, she ran in that direction while the bear hobbled after her. She sped through the thick growth. Springing branches and sharp twigs scratched and bloodied her and tugged on her long black, flowing hair. Then a low-lying, thorny twig caught her by the hem of her dress and stopped her in her tracks. She struggled to get free, while the bear gained on her. The threatening groans and thundering steps of the big bear caused her heart to pound. She tugged desperately on her dress. As the bear rose on its haunches ready to claw her, a flying pick-axe struck its belly with a thud as it did not penetrate. But it was enough to stun the bear and he scurried off on all fours grunting and moaning all the way ran back to its cave.

The eighth little man slid down the tree and ran to free the princess from the clutches of the stubborn twig. The princess smiled and her beautiful teeth glowed pearly pink in the early dawn. She patted his funny looking hat and said, "Oh, thank you, my little man, for saving my life. It seemed the bear wanted me for its breakfast."

"Oh, yes, they do not turn away from meat when they stumble on it, but most of the time they are content with the many fruits and berries of our woods," squeaked the little man. Then he stuck out his bony chest and proudly added, forgetting his shame of the previous day, "It is my honor to have saved such a beautiful girl as you."

She blushed and said modestly, "I am honored that you feel honored. As for being beautiful, though I think of myself as plain, it appears that is my problem. My stepmother, anyway, thinks I am at least becoming beautiful, and because of it, tried to have me killed. You see, she is indeed very beautiful but apparently no one else can be."

The dwarf scratched through his hat and said, looking puzzled,

"Why how can that be? For no one who is truly beautiful could deny beauty in another!"

"Ah, but you do not know the jealous queen."

"Queen?" he echoed. "Then you must be the lovely Snow White— why, of course, who else would have such ruby lips, shining black hair and skin as white as snow!" he added, thinking of the reflection in the coin last night. "Yes, yes, no other could you be than the daughter of our dear departed and true queen."

She looked kindly and wistfully at the little man while turning her thoughts to her true mother." You are not only brave and honorable but kind and gentle as well."

He blushed and wished that his fraternity of dwarfs had thought so too.

She leaned over and kissed each of his red cheeks. He flushed so that his entire face, including his ears, became as red as his cheeks. She giggled over his bashfulness, then said, "Oh, my little knight, forgive me if I embarrassed you by my gratitude for saving my life!…Now, since you know my name, you must tell me yours."

"I'm called Ahto."

"Otto?"

"No, Snow White, not Otto,….*Ah*-too.

Snow White held back her laughter and covered her smile. "My, what an unusual name!" Then she thought better of it, and added, "Rather charming in fact."

He flushed again, then took her soft delicate hand in his rough, pudgy one. At that moment he felt more guilty than when his theft was discovered because he wished that he could kiss that lovely hand. He quickly withdrew his hand and gestured that she follow him. Ahto led her to a spring and washed her scratches and the blood streaks from her face and hands. Miraculously the scratches disappeared and her face indeed was again as pure as snow. He removed the large gold, coin from his pocket and it glittered in the

35

rising sun. He held it up to her like a mirror so she could see her image. "There now," he said, "is proof of your beauty. There is no one fairer than you."

She blushed at the magical reflection, then chuckled. "Tell that to the queen and her magic mirror, Alto." She looked again into the strange gold piece and was surprised to see she was wearing a beautiful comb. She touched the top of her head but there was no comb. She looked again and saw an image of her figure and round her waist she wore a lace of gold that highlighted a beautiful satin dress. She looked down but she wore no lace round her bodice, and she was in her soiled, torn garment. She glanced at the dwarf and in a puzzled tone said, "Oh, why show me these beautiful things when I shall never have them now that I am forever to dwell under forest trees or in caves meant for bears? Alas, I am abandoned and alone. No house, much less beautiful things."

"Ah, but you are not alone. I am here and shall watch over you whenever you venture out from the house to gather berries," he said to comfort her.

"House! What house?...The house the woodsman mentioned?" She looked at him wide-eyed and handed him the coin.

"Why, the cottage of my brothers in kind. They are honorable and hard working men who will care for you until you come of age and marry a handsome prince," he assured her, putting the coin back in his pocket. Then he quickly pulled it out again, polished it on his coat collar and handed it back to her. "You keep it, Snow White. One as pretty as you should have a mirror. My brothers are so ugly — as you can imagine by casting your sparkling eyes on me — that there is no mirror in the cottage."

She sparkled with gaiety and said anxiously, "How kind you are—and to me also very handsome." she kissed him again on his blushing cheek, then said, "Then take me to your home and I shall cook and clean for you and your brothers."

"I shall show you the way, but I am no longer permitted to live there," he said sadly. "But I promise to watch over you should you wander in the forest. And if you cannot find me just flash the coin to the top of the second of seven mountains and I shall appear and guide you to the finest fruit in the kingdom to quell your hunger, then escort you back to the house."

He led her to the narrow path and walked awhile with her till the little cottage was in his vision. He stopped and pointed to the house, then bade her farewell, but she held him by the collar and begged, "Please, my little knight, do not go. I shall speak up for you, Ahto, and am sure that your brothers will forgive you for whatever you have done."

He touched her smooth white hand to release his collar and said, thoughtfully, "You are indeed a princess and will make a great and beautiful queen as your natural mother was. I thank you for your warm, kind feeling but I must go to explore the seven mountains to find my worth. For it is said that when one does wrong and knows that he has, he must make amends to regain his true self." He briefly, gently squeezed her hand and then scampered off on his short skinny legs.

Saddened by his departure, she walked along the widening path to the cottage of the now seven dwarfs. She removed the golden disk tucked in her bodice. The magical light, equaling the depth and intensity of her stepmother's magic looking glass, reflected sharply the treetops and the sky. Then a bright red apple—red as her lips—appeared but out of which a worm worked its way and transformed into an evil looking witch. Thankfully, the witch gave way to a view of the mountains and then only the second of the seven mountains. There in the tree standing almost tall upon a branch was Ahto looking through a telescope. Suddenly from behind the seven mountains appeared another: Thrusting skyward from the new mountain side was a magnificent ebony castle—as dark as the

37

frame of her mother's once beautiful portrait that her stepmother had painted over and replaced with her magic mirror. The tower roofs sparkled a snowy white, topped with ruby-red flags.

The image faded as she approached the house and the gold piece grew cold in her hand. After admiring the quaintness of the cottage and smelling the many flowers surrounding it, she was about to enter when a great flood of sunlight enveloped her. She felt the gold in her hand grow warm again. Impulsively she opened her hand and the golden disk glowed brighter than before. She looked into it. The eighth dwarf was smiling at her and then he faded. Suddenly a fine white horse was sculpted into the piece right before her eyes. Then Ahto bedecked in royal garb mounted it. As he straddled the white horse, the dwarf grew in stature and Ahto changed into the legendary handsome, charming prince of tall tales. And the magic gold piece was forever minted in the likeness of the prince of Snow White's impression.

"Hm, I wonder." Snow White murmured to herself. She fondled the coin, then tucked it away and reached for the door. She hesitated and thought, " Of course, why not? After all, if a frog can change into a prince…" She giggled and went inside the cottage of the Seven Dwarfs.

First City State

A hundred thousand years of science, mathematics and intra-solar system flight was the trademark of an ancient planet circling a star that hung on the fringe of a galaxy so distant that it actually scraped against the shell of space. Ultimately its inhabitants discovered that the space-time continuum was but an invention fashioned out of the limitations of their own perceptual mechanics. After mega calculations and tedious conditioning, they were able to jump out of space and time at will and then choose any point in the physical universe.

Sixty million years ago in obsolescent time when the dinosaur roamed the corners of the earth, a great spaceship jumped back into a designated point in the continuum, spread out its immense retractable wings, swooped into the thick cosmic dust and landed on a rolling plain of rich soil, still millions of years from becoming a desert. For now, the relatively young earth — in non-geological terms — was everywhere still tropical from its boiling insides spewing steam and cleansing the murky atmosphere that had been trapping the heat for three and a half billion years.

Except for life-support adjustments by officers in the saucer-like command tower set back and above the nose, by earth's measure of time in the context of human standards several weeks passed before there was general activity from the sleek ship's four hundred-foot swept-back wings serving as living quarters whether extended or retracted from the enormous cylindrical fuselage housing equipment and provisions. Once adjusted to the new sense of gravity, the explorers ventured out in small groups to breathe in the new air and to test their agility to heavier gravity than they were used to. Each earth day the crew and passengers would step down and mill round the ship to take in more air until their space manager deduced from the ship's computers that the new inhabitants had safely adjusted to a natural state for this particular planet.

Ramps protruded from the belly of the ship, and an array of robotic construction-machinery emerged — some on steel belt-cleats, some on tires with deeply cut treads, others on talon-like feet — to begin the development of the very first city-state. These

39

immense robots busied about as the great beasts of the era seemed to look on with curiosity while bathing in the river that cut through a terrain already beginning to show signs of large sand deposits. The larger dinosaurs even felt intimidated by these strange moving objects — never before having perceived anything mobile larger than themselves. But the most intimidating was the band of defensive warriors issuing from the ship. Equipped with an assortment of weapons, designed merely to make noise and flashing light, these exploring defenders harmlessly herded the mighty beasts away from the construction project.

Swiftly and methodically the robots sculpted smooth blocks from cosmic debris and volcanic rock deposited some billion years before and erected a forty-foot high wall for two thousand feet circumventing the spaceship while the settlers assisted by smaller robots began constructing shelters from materials unloaded from the ship.

An occasional brontosaurus, while dining off leaves of tall trees whose branches hung over the mighty wall, would peer over at the strange biped creatures who industriously yet with carefree mannerism would work among their robots whose larger counterparts were now busily clearing vegetation from along the river. No "earth" creature — the new arrivals labeled the planet Trinus — small or large had ever before witnessed a living, tail-less thing so proportionately erect and agile as these Trinians. Even the fearsome tyrannosaur, in spite of its incredible speed, could hardly produce with the ease of fish the twists, turns and spurts of energy, along with the incredible maneuverability of the upper limbs of these new arrivals of early "man."

So efficient were the new masters of Trinus that before the moon could complete its cycle, the settlement within the city wall was complete. The aliens — now fully aware that they were to be permanent natives — turned their attention to outside the wall where they began in unison with the smaller robots to farm the land while the defenders kept the native animals at a distance, rather than kill them, since seldom did the aliens have to hunt them down for food. Their computer in light of the reptiles' immensity estimated that one kill would suffice the settlers' protein for two cycles of the moon. Of course, there was sufficient processed nourishment aboard ship, but which would soon be returning to the home planet for another exploration assignment. Those left behind possessed the knowledge to produce the processed nourishment. However, in spite of the supracivilization to which they were accustomed, these Trinians would never lose the taste for natural foods as a matter of pride and celebration of life. Even before the major project for which they came began, giant silos were beginning to tower over the beds of the trickling stream.

This celebration ironically was in direct contrast to the profession that most of these adult settlers practiced: succeeding generations of Trinians would nonetheless perpetuate for a million years. The advent of a great cosmic accident here would force these space creatures to take up residence elsewhere in another young solar system like our own in order to perpetrate the dictum from their overcrowded home planet of agéd inhabitants. By that time, however, they would have grown so attached to Trinus that they would nostalgically intuit that their descendants thousands of generations beyond the coming cataclysm would return— consistent with their venturesome heritage—to restore Trinian intelligence to this hapless, brutish globe.

These pre-cataclysmic ancestors of human origin, in spite of their prevailing profession, had not lost touch with agrarian practice. It reminded them of the natural beauty in the cycles of life and therefore worked the new soil with gusto, knowing that soon most of them would no longer have the time to recreate in this time-honored activity of birth, generation and yield for harvest.

41

For, only the evening before, after having checked on the progress of the giant robots working by the now surging stream from the south, the space manager had assembled the unit-heads of the profession to the freshly completed city-hall to announce that the first hearse ship was to arrive: whereupon they would be embalming the shipment from the old home before interring the remains in the first pyramid constructed along the young river.

The Little Flower Girl

Thousands of years ago in the ancient city of Athens there was a little flower girl whom all citizens had drawn her into their hearts. No one knew whence she came, for she would appear each sunny morning on a ray of dawn. At the close of the day she would ride the pink stretches of sunset and fade into the shadows of dusk. So lovely in her manner was this little girl that Athenians of all walks of life had commented at one time or another that she must have been born of the gods. So lovely to look at was she that many said she was more beautiful than the freshly picked flowers she would generously offer them with dancing eyes and a pearly smile. Her hair was brighter than the golden daffodils that graced her handsome basket that they say was woven in Ithaca by the loyal Penelope herself. Her skin was whiter than the snowy lilies she gathered by the stream of nymphs. Her eyes were more sparkling than the bluest hyacinths she grew in the fabled garden of

Hyacinthus.

When she approached the temples, many claimed they had actually seen smiles across the stone faces of the many statues of the gods she — raised up by tall citizens — would grace with freshly made wreaths. All of the Athenians had sworn that they had heard a lyre play and the singing of the Muse whenever she would approach the gleaming Parthenon and place the choicest lily from her basket before the city's most beloved goddess, Athena, who was worshiped for her passion for justice.

One day in front of the graceful statue of Aphrodite, the goddess of love and beauty, the little flower girl was gently twisting the long stems of daffodils to form lovely golden wreath. When done she asked a tall boy to climb up onto the smooth marble pedestal and place the wreath upon the head of the beautiful goddess. As the little flower girl looked up to admire the golden crown, Aphrodite from Mount Olympus looked down and was pleased with what the child had done. So pleased was she that she jumped into her ivory chariot, tapped the reins to signal a silvery horse to descend from the home of the gods.

When the beauty-goddess softly landed in the city's square framed by majestic temples, she was disappointed that no one paid any attention to her arrival. Instead the Athenians were gathered admiringly round the little flower girl who was happily and charitably handing out flowers to them from the magical basket that seemingly had no bottom. Not only had they not noticed the goddess, they did not even seem to notice the crown upon her statue. "*Some* day of flattery this is!" she snickered under her breath. "No wonder Athena so often walks among them invisible, lest they mock her for her silly helmet, shield and spear."

The goddess moved through the crowd and saw close up how beautiful indeed was this child. Aphrodite was proud until she observed that the Athenians were admiring the child more than the

43

flowers she was handing them. Aphrodite's soft emerald eyes rolled to the murky seaweed green of envy. The goddess moved in even closer to the girl and then heard an old woman say to the child, "My dear child of soft and endless petals, the golden crown of daffodils on the head of our goddess of beauty belongs upon your golden head!"

Aphrodite was so enraged by the woman's remark that she abruptly turned on her heels and headed for her chariot. Her long white silky robe was swirling in the winds of her mean emotions.

The little girl in disbelief looked at the old woman. "Oh, no!" cried the girl with an embarrassed smile. "It is because of the very charm of our beautiful goddess that you say that. Aphrodite makes us see beauty in everything and in everyone."

The goddess did not hear the girl's answer; nor, so swept up in envy, would it have mattered. She cracked a whip across the flanks of her silvery horse and it lunged skyward. She then wrenched back on the rein, and the chariot hovered momentarily over the child. From the tip of her long slender finger the jealous goddess released a bolt of anger at the little girl's heart. To the horror of the citizens, the child in a puff of green smoke disappeared before their shocked, bulging eyes. Only the basket of flowers remained.

The old woman went to the basket and retrieved a lily and held it to her heart. Later at home she would press it into her scroll of myths in memory of the child. Others too took flowers to remember her by, for they feared they would never again see their precious little flower girl. A wise old man took the basket home with him. The next day he went to see the city's most famous sculptor. He asked the sculptor to make a statue of the little flower girl. The sculptor was delighted, for he had often seen her, whose kindness and loveliness were alive in his memory.

Months later, on the day the city was to celebrate the goddess of beauty, the sculptor unveiled a marble image of the little flower girl.

Hundreds of Athenians gathered and were happy to see the lovely statue; yet their sadness lingered. Even though the pure white marble was as white as her pearly skin, it could not emit her living radiance. The wise old man approached the new statue and placed before it the handsome basket, and the old woman came forth to fill it with fresh hyacinths, daffodils and lilies, though not of the highest quality that the little flower girl would have mysteriously gathered.

Aphrodite descended from her resting crag at Olympus to revel in her day of honor. When she saw the statue of the little flower girl, her eyes fired green heat of envy before the red flame of rage erupted over the insult. She looked up to the great mountain in the clouds and shrilled to her husband, the god of crafts. Instantly Hephæstus went to work at his anvil and forged a heavy iron hammer. Then he tossed it down into her hand. With hideous shrieks and unladylike grunts and crunching swoops, she smashed the statue to white sand. Swirling round, her robe trailing wildly in the fury, she roared in disgust at the

Athenians and hurled the hammer into the crowd. Fortunately the citizens scattered unharmed. She tossed the flowers to the winds of insults and climbed into her chariot. She bolted for Mount Olympus to sulk away her day of honor.

The crowd gathered round the mound of dust, whose prior shape had been briefly their source of joy. The proud sculptor was now bent over, weeping at a handful of marble dust he had gently scooped up. All of the Athenians began to moan and weep for their living joy.

Athena, the city's most honorable spirit, observing the scene below, took pity on her loving Athenians who were now so steeped in sadness. She took up her shield and spear and strode toward Hephæstus' workshop, behind which she knew she would find her jealous sister.

45

Aphrodite was sitting on a crag, her knees up. She was still steaming from rage, glaring down upon the weeping city. She cried out with venom, "Yea, weep your heart out — O sentimental mankind! Yea, weep for a child of your fancy. Yea, turn against me in whom you once rejoiced in the true beauty of myself whom you now ignore!" Athena approached and heard. She said to her sister, "I once thought that in you, my dear sister, there indeed was true beauty. So much beauty and so gracious were you that I had nothing but admiration and love for you. Never once was I jealous of your beauty and your extraordinary ability to love. Never once did I resent the affection and praise showered upon you by our family of deities and humanity.... Too, I was sensible enough to thank our blessings for the beauty you brought forth to the world. And so, too, do my Athenians count their blessings for the beauty and love you have sent to my fair city. Yes, their love of beauty and sense of love itself with your help brought forth that lovely flower girl. Yes, that child is as much your doing as theirs. For you inspired them to appreciate all beauty. And yet here you sulk like a spoiled little nymph unable to accept your very own gift to the world. You gave and then cruelly took away."

Aphrodite's hard look dissolved from her sister's wise words. Her soft emerald eyes returned as she glanced up and said, "You say, you once thought of me as true beauty,... but no longer?"

"Alas, that's true." Athena admitted with lowered eyes but then slowly raised them, looking softly at her sister and touching her lovely face, now wrinkled by self-willed torment. "For how can there be beauty in you when you loathe it in others?"

Aphrodite flared with momentary anger, and said, "That's simply not true!" Her anger subsided and she said softly, "Why, I love you and see in you a beauty far superior to mine, for you have the beauty of reason."

"Oh?...And am I to think that because you are beautiful you

46

cannot be reasonable?" Athena asked, showing disappointment. Then thrusting the spear harmlessly, she added, "Must I threaten to scar you with my spear before you release the dear little girl from your powers of jealousy?"

Aphrodite flinched, then giggled. "Oh, dear Athena, though you are known for your stern justice, you could not harm a hair on my head." She brushed aside the spear, gently removed her sister's helmet and kissed her on the cheek. "As always your words ring of truth. Indeed, I am acting as a spoiled child in being envious of another, especially of that dear, sweet child." Taking her sister's hands in hers, Aphrodite with contrition in her heart and shame in her glance, confessed, "Yea, 'tis true; I did create her for your loving people to remind them daily that there resided love and beauty in their own hearts."

Athena smiled with compassion and said, "Then why when they expressed what was in their hearts, were you upset so?"

"I honestly don't know—oh, I suppose you would call it a childish temper of envy—yet somehow I suspected the people would react as they had."

"Ah, is it not rare among deities, my darling Aphrodite!" Athena inferred, touching her sister's damp cheek. "Don't you see? It is the ageless dilemma of affection for the created or for the creator." Aphrodite looked askance then lowered her lids in shame. "Yea, I do see. Thus envy rode the horns and broke the natural flow of reason you had given them to resolve such perplexities."

Said the wise sister, "Indeed, for they — and especially the little darling flower girl — would have seen that the Mover and the Moved are one and the same."

Aphrodite hugged her sister and felt the heartbeat of Athena tirelessly pumping the sweet liquid of justice to the valleys of man. She stepped away and looked into her sister's honey-brown eyes.

47

Aphrodite's glacial heart once more admitted the warm flow of love for humankind. She stroked her sister's long soft hair that matched the honey color of her eyes. "Oh, Athena, it is *you* who are truly beautiful!" Then she giggled. "But why, must you wear that silly armor?"

"Only to guard against the fanciful whims of my darling but unpredictable sister," Athena snapped, then burst a chuckling smile.

Aphrodite laughed heartily. Then said seriously, "Still, I am not so spoiled that I cannot see my errant ways when you challenge me with your unrelenting wisdom."

She swirled round on the edge of the crag and a cloud of green appeared; it swooped down the mountain side onto the city and landed on the empty pedestal but for the mound of white sand. The dark green cloud brightened to her sister's honey gold across the tear-filled eyes of the Athenians below. Suddenly their eyes dried and popped from a gusty wind centrifuging the green cloud now sucking up the marble dust. The dust of love and beauty forged an arch of flowers, upon which glowed the brightest rays that Aphrodite could urge from Apollo. The Athenians gasped in wonder and anticipation as flower petals of every description wafted out to them from the floral arch. They cheered, cried, hugged and shook hands when out stepped the little flower girl — her skin as warm and radiant as the lily she had presented to Athena's image, her eyes as blue as proud petals from the garden of Hyacinthus. And her hair was as bright as Apollo's rays; even more so because Aphrodite had crowned *her* with a wreath of golden daffodils.

Jill And The Banana Tree

While staying with her grandmother in Florida during Christmas vacation, Jill often sat under a banana tree in the backyard, which had no other shade trees. At first Jill did not believe it was a banana tree because it had no bananas growing from it until her grandmother explained that even in the sub-tropics there was a fruit season. This saddened her since she only visited her grandmother in the winter and she did so wish to experience the sight of real bananas growing above her.

One day her grandmother and grandfather took her to the zoo. At the monkey cage a sprightly baby monkey jumped all around when it saw her. It jumped on the trapeze and began to swing back and forth by the tail. It swung harder and harder until the baby monkey got close to the wire and then stretched its arm out toward Jill. It seemed to have something in its hand. It squealed each time it got close to her as though it were trying to say something to her. The next time it came close, it tapped the hand holding the object with the other. On the next arc it jumped for the screen and held on, then passed a dried-out banana peel through the screen. Jill took it and somehow understood.

She could not wait to get back to the house. She ran to the banana tree and placed the peel on one of its massive foliage branches and sat down. She looked up expecting something to happen. Instead the banana peel slid down the trunk to the base. Jill thought of burying it near the root, but thought better of it because then she would not be able to see it anymore. She ran back in the house and retrieved a knife. She walked back to the tree carefully because she remembered that her mother cautioned her about running while carrying sharp instruments. She slit the thin bark in two places to make a band, then carefully lifted it and slipped the

49

banana peel underneath. She sat down and gazed at it for a half hour but nothing happened. She heard her grandmother calling and she went inside for supper.

After supper she helped her grandmother clean up, after which they both sat down to watch TV. During a commercial Jill asked, "Nana, do you think next summer I could come down to visit?"

"Oh, I don't think your mother would like that idea. You have that special summer school, don't forget. And they would want you home for when they go off on vacation to the mountains. You wouldn't like it down here — it's much too hot."

"Oh, but I so much want to see the banana tree with bananas!" The grandmother chuckled. "Maybe if I picked them young and green I could send them priority mail, and I'll send you pictures of it — if we're still here."

"Nana, what do you mean!" Jill always worried about their health and shuddered to think of her life without them.

"No, my child, not that. It's just that living on social security and Gramps little pension makes it very hard to make ends meet and we may be forced to sell the house and move to a small condo or trailer park."

"Oh, dear, will you be able to take the tree?"

"Oh, I'm afraid not."

The grandfather came from another room and said, "Mary, I'm going to the store to buy another lottery ticket."

"Oh, John, not again! We can't afford it. It's becoming an obsession with you. If we lose the house, so be it. Life will go on."

Jill jumped out of the chair. "Oh, Gramps, can I go with you? I have a dollar you can have."

"Of course, you can come with me. But I'm not going to use your dollar."

"I should hope not!" the grandmother said. "Such a thing for a little girl."

"Then I'll use it myself," Jill protested.

"Certainly not," the grandmother disagreed. "Besides, it's illegal."

"Then Gramps can do it for me," Jill reasoned.

"End the subject, Jill," the grandmother ordered firmly. "Go with your grandfather, if you like — just forget your silly notions."

Inside the supermarket at the special counter for Lotto, Jill stared up at the sign of big numbers. She started counting the zeros. "Wow," she squealed, "Ten million!"

"Yep, Jill," the grandfather said, "that will keep us in our house for quite a spell."

"Forever, Gramps!"

The grandfather stood over the writing desk pondering his choices. He had been mixing up his combinations so much that he could no longer think straight. He always used birthdays starting with the grandchildren. One time he'd go by how old some of them were then include his own children's ages. Next the days they were born, then months and years. He could not remember what he chose last time. "What did it matter? It's only chance, anyway. Maybe I should let their computer pick them."

Then he looked down at Jill. "Honey, promise me you won't tell Nana if I ask you to pick the numbers."

Her eyes glittered as she stretched a smile, then quickly covered up her braces. "I promise, Gramps, but not when we win. I'd be too excited and know I'll slip on a banana!"

Gramps laughed. "Honey, if you win, I don't think anyone will mind — including your puritan grandmother." He poised the pencil. "Okay, Jill, what'll they be." She didn't even have to think, rattling them off too quickly for him to fill in the card. "Oh, the quickness of young minds!...Now, take it slow."

She repeated them slowly, but steadily without reservation, "3-14-15-21-18-10."

"Goodness, and not one of our birthdays!" Gramps said, truly

51

amazed. "Pretty low numbers, though. How could you have come up with them so fast if you weren't thinking of birthdays?"

She winked and smiled. "Actually they just popped in." Which was true but now she knew why.

In the car on the way home, Jill said to him, "You won't sell the house when you win, Gramps, will you?" He laughed. "No fear of that, darlin ' The whole point of it is to keep the house....And, of course, my granddaughter's banana tree." He winked at her. "So, you're pretty sure, huh?...Not even 'if' but 'when'. That's wonderful, honey; don't ever lose the hope of the young.... Anyway, if you win, will *you* let me keep the house?"

"Oh, Gramps,...it was your dollar."

"Nevertheless, after the house the rest goes into trust for all the grandchildren." Then he winked again, chuckled and added, "With a big bonus for you."

The next day she ran to the banana tree. There was no sign of growth; yet she blinked her eyes twice: the peel she slid under the bark was a much brighter yellow. "Hm, maybe it means by the time I leave there will be the seed of the mother flower — at least I'll get to see that."

Later in the day after she helped Gramps with the lawn. While he mowed, she ran the electric weed trimmer under the watchful eye of her nervous Nana. Afterwards, she took a dip in the pool and then relaxed under her tree. She almost dosed off when a bird flew under the fan-like branches and lighted on the juncture and began to peck at the peel that had now taken on a sheen. She raised herself up; the bird flew off. She looked closely. With her fingernail she flicked the peel. It had grown hard, almost plastic or metallic; the edges of the peel had curled up giving a tiny cup-like appearance, resembling one of the pieces to her dollhouse tea-set. She was disappointed because it did not look like a seedling of any kind — she was hoping there would be a sign of petals that would turn more green or perhaps even wine-red, the color of the mother flower.

She went back into her room to read her loosely bound book of fairy tales. Before she started she had to tape back in some of the pages that were barely hanging in. At the point where Jack threw the beans out the window, she got up to close the door as the background of her grandparents discussion in the next room was beginning to distract her. As she closed it, she heard her grandfather bemoan, "Two months,...is about it....Then we'll have to sell. Taxes are killing us."

Sunday morning after church and breakfast, Jill ducked under the massive tree branches, one of the heavy trunks bent severely. Her eyes popped at the heavy cluster of red-wine flowers of the mother. Right above it were tiny tips of green baby bananas, golden tip of one shone. She clapped her hands and pushed away a giant leaf and ran onto the patio where her grandparents were reading the Sunday paper, screeching, "Gramps, we won, won!"

"Calm down, Jill,...Gracious!" Her Nana pleaded.

But Jill could not control herself. She looked over at her grandfather and screeched excitedly, "Gramps, the paper...you never looked in the paper?"

Gramps put down the paper and looked up quizzically, "Huh?...Oh, Lotto...my, I clean forgot!"

He reached for the first page section on the table and looked in the lower corner; he blinked his eyes, took off his glasses, wiped them with the tail of his sports shirt, put them back on. His hand shook; he handed the paper to Jill. "Impossible...I need your young eyes." He squinted and squeezed her little hand.

Jill looked: up popped 3-14-15-21-18-10. "I knew it!" she screamed. "Banana Tree!"

"Huh?" Gramps grunted.

"Don't you see? $B+A=3, N=14, A+N=15, A+T=21, R=18, E+E=10$ — ten letters for ten million!"

Gramps yelped, "Unbelievable — beats the birthday formula!" He picked her up in his arms, swung her round. "A genius for a granddaughter!" He put her down and pulled his wife from the chair and danced her round the patio.

Nana felt dizzy and sat back down. She heaved, "Shame on you for letting her gamble."

Jill, giggling, said, "Oh, it wasn't gambling, Nana; it was monkeyshine!"

Lonely Planet

Many billions of years ago the sun, called Sol, was still a playful youngster skipping near and round other stars in the vast Milky Way. To his sadness many of the larger playmates, even though they used to bully him, had grown up so that they were busy making playmates or planets for themselves.

Then Sol turned to the younger stars to idle in Great Time, but soon he tired of their childish manner; for all they wanted to play was shooting star, a game that exhausted him, requiring long dashes into the darkest regions of the universe. And because he was not a bully himself, Sol could not force them to play the game he liked most, which was to blow solar winds at star dust to form beautiful star crystals and icy bubbles.

Sol became discouraged and returned to his own colorless yard. For some time he plopped himself in the middle of a neutral void and did nothing but broil in his own disappointment and sadness. Suddenly a sense of shame stirred in him and a feeling of responsibility boiled up inside and steamed away some of his youthful ways. "Ah," he bellowed to the empty yard, "I hear Nature's voice calling — I too must make a world!" Then he began to spin like a top, giggling to the four corners of his yard: "I'll turn my work to play!" And as Sol spun faster and faster great balls of fire jumped off his belly and spiraled off in different directions as though playing hide-'n'-seek. "Yes, yes, playmates, enjoy — but I cannot have you scattering about here and there. I shall have to put you on a carousel and I at the center will see that you won't fall off and hurt yourselves by bumping into nearby, mischievous asteroids. Oh, what a joyous time we'll have till the end of our time. A jolly merry-go-round in my play yard!"

The smaller ones were no match for the giant balls hurling through space, leaving them far behind. The smallest one felt so insecure that it did not dare venture much beyond Sol, for fear it would lose its native warmth in such cold blackness of space. The tiny flaming ball started to circle under Sol's wagging tongue and was content to hear the solar music of the carousel. Three — all of similar size — journeyed off, but a very beautiful one bedecked in silvery robes, the younger sister of the new born family, turned round to her baby brother and took pity. Her bright eyes turned to tears as she edged back to be near the little one and hovered round it to be sure it did not get too close to Sol. She warned, "Mind now, little Mercury, enjoy the music but lo, do not get lapped up by Sol's hot tongue!"

The other two jaunted off thinking they could catch up with their brawny brothers far beyond them. But in a little while the older sister began to grow cool and turn white, then blue and stopped in her track. "Don't go too far, dear brother, or you will lose Sol's warming rays." "Bah, that's nonsense!" cried the other. Why, I'm as fiery red as when I started! And just look at our bigger brothers — why they're glowing as mightily as big Sol!"

"Maybe," said the blue one, "but it's awfully cold out here and I don't think it's wise to go too far. Stay here with me and be my escort. I tell you, I feel where we are is just the right place on this heavenly merry-go-round."

The red, younger brother laughed. "How can there be any fun when so close to the middle. No, it is more thrilling to be on the outside, so we can really f eel the breeze on our face as our father swings us round. Of course, those big bullies will take the best

55

sections on the outer rim; still, I'll stay close to them and get the better thrill of the ride than you!"

"Don't go too far," the blue sister warned. "Why, look behind you. Our dear silvery sister seems already so far away, watching after our baby brother."

The red one wobbled and gnarled dark channels in his red face. "That's because she is so proud of her beauty and wants to stand out from the rest of us. Look, already she is dancing round, twinkling brighter than the stars! And look at yourself — why, as vain as our young sister — already you're traipsing about spinning a glorious blue and white mantle as though you were a proud queen!"

"I told you I was cold out here. I am not about to circle this dreaded darkness naked! Please stay with me."

The brother bounced like a red ball and laughed. "No fear, I promise not to go too far, and my great red flames will keep you toasty warm." He then threw out a ball of fire to her. "Just to be sure keep this by your side." And he bounced away to catch up with the others. His mighty brothers were too far away, so as promised he stayed close to his big sister.

The other four continued their mad dash to the fringe of the yard. Each bumping each other, struggling to be the first at the outer edge. But the largest one no longer could pull his weight. Tuckered out and gasping for breath he rolled to a stop and started shaking beads of sweat that crystallized round him from the frigid blackness. So cold were they and so close to the redheaded brother that his flaming youth turned to dark red embers as he desperately blew the crystals back to his giant brother. Thirteen icy crystals finally shaped themselves into smaller spheres and settled round the fattest brother.

Suddenly Sol's winds coughed up a myriad of flaming dust and they landed round the other huge brother further out, and like a lariat they entwined him as they turned to ice. He, too, froze and could jump no more; like a huge roped bull he was corralled by the circular path. With the icy twine about his middle he watched resentfully while his other two brothers raced for the corner post of the yard.

Though the stronger of the remaining two was way in front, he slid on an ice crystal and started tumbling into orbit as the other took command of the outer edge. As this weaker brother sailed rapidly round the far reaches of Sol's powerful pull, he was sorry that he had dashed so far out. He shivered from the icy winds, and his flame turned to ice cycles, then he turned blue and started to crack. A piece of his shoulder fell off and drifted for a moment until Sol's sling shot action hurled it further into space beyond even Sol's great muscular gravitational pull. Without having a chance to shape itself into a smooth sphere, the poor, hapless chunk of icy shoulder drifted for billions of years between two worlds heading toward another star.

Finally the great force of the nearest star dragged it into another yard wondrously aglow with giant star crystals whose warmth began to melt the icy stranger. Its inborn, dormant flame erupted and it began to swirl into a shining sphere and a warm smile crossed the new, tiny planet's flaming face.

A huge planet seeing this strange intruder broke from its orbit and approached. It had never seen anything so small. The tiny planet had never seen anything so big and hot other than Sol. "Surely," the tiny intruder thought, "it was twice the size of his biggest brother at home!" "You are trespassing!" the giant bellowed. "If you are not out of here before I roll back into orbit, I shall lap out at you and swallow you up."

"But why, great one? I am so small. I promise not to get in your way and surely there is plenty of room in this grand yard."

"Indeed there is but that's not the point. Look all around you. What do you see?"

"My, how unbelievable! Except for the warm star crystals that keep the home-fires burning, I swear I do see you — thousands of you!" He looked again and squealed, "By my big brother Jove, I think I see a thousand me's, too!"

"Precisely. My ruling sun is vain and lazy. Instead of creating a thousand different planets he spewed out endless icy mirrors and just one me. If he catches you he will get mad and shatter all the mirrors and then I shall be alone."

"But he will be happy that I'm here to keep you company!"the little planet replied with a pleading tone.

"No, as I said, he is a lazy, vain sun and will not tolerate caring for another playmate. He will simply tuck you in his hydrogen pocket and you will be no more."

"If I leave I am no more, but odd shaped and lost forever in the blackness, better to be in his pocket — at least I shall be warm." "Ah, but you won't know that because you will melt down and therefore be nothing."

"I shall be nothing out there in the horrible darkness!" he cried. "Nothing but a horribly deformed chunk of ice suspended between my yard and yours."

"No, I shall send with you one of our star crystal sentries to escort you back to your yard. You will remain a flaming ball, however tiny, and when you arrive at your cold yard's orbit you will crystalize into a beautiful, smooth snowball that will be the envy of your playmates." "Oh, my, how kind of you, and yet I know not your name," the little lonely planet squealed.

The giant ball bounced jovially as he left his tiny ward, and answered, "Bluto."

Thus, the lonely little planet was carried with speed from the solar system of mirrors to his own family yard by the warmly smiling crystal. Sol was happy for his return, having regretted tossing him away in anger. He set him in an interesting orbit so he wouldn't be bored and feel alone anymore — the little planet was especially thrilled when he could meet up with his brother whose chipped shoulder was responsible for his being.

And thus, missing from the astronomers' search of Sol's grand garden for thousands of years, little Pluto was finally discovered.

Princess Amanda

In a kingdom somewhere long, long ago, a princess, nearing her twenty-first birthday, strolled onto a balcony that adjoined her private rooms midway up the castle tower. Leaning over an ornate balustrade

she gazed wistfully down at morning activity of the castle wards. She particularly observed all the lovely maidens that had gathered at the central well to draw the day's water for the nobility. The princess let out deep sighs and wished that she could join them, though knowing that could never be:

For, one day when she was about fifteen she had attempted joining a similar gathering. The princess had disguised herself by upbraiding her hair — her one apparent redeeming feature — and over it a long, coarse wig covering most of her countenance. Then she put on tattered clothing and peasant sandals. She slipped out from the back end of the donjon stairs, smeared some dust from the ward on her stick-like legs, feet and bony cheeks and headed for the well where young maidens had gathered at the offspring used for laundering.

The princess tried to mingle, but the girls ignored her with cruel pretense of being too busy — nonetheless, casting glances at her, then back to each other either to giggle, raise a brow to snicker or drop a jaw to gape. However mean they were, the princess still admired them for their natural beauty. Even while doing menial work they seemed so delicate, so feminine. She offered to help a pretty girl with the laundry. The girl, who was not much older than the princess, rejected her in a huff. An older girl with gorgeous long red hair and enviable, sparkling green eyes, lashed out with a wet shirt and hit the princess on the arm. They all laughed when the intruder screeched out of surprise than hurt.

"Off with you, you dirty girl," said the redhead, "you dip those filthy hands in the spring and you'll dirty our wash." She knew the redhead very well, and the surprise assault did turn to heartfelt hurt. The girls all laughed again and then even harder when the wig parted, revealing her large bulbous nose. They all began to jeer her when they took in her appearance as though for the first time. Some went into convulsive laughter when they stared at her squinty eyes too small and her mouth too big for a her long drawn face; they gawked at her all too noticeable veiny hands attached to angular arms, along with her gangling limbs, adding to the enormity of her large feet and stubby toes. The cord round her tunic disclosed a tiny waist which was, however, unfavorably juxtaposed to bony shoulders framed as wide as a knight's in armor.

Cruelly the maidens — including the red hair beauty who now surmised her identity — kept up their jeering and howling while each took turns taunting her by squinting their eyes, pulling on their lips, tweaking her nose, stepping on her feet, mocking the measurement of her shoulders until a young knight who was witnessing this cruel frolicking rushed to the poor girl's defense.

He chastised the silly maidens, ordering them to go on with their work. He took by the hand the poor girl, who was by now tearful and sobbing, and led her to the outer ward of the peasantry where he assumed she belonged.

"Dear lass, you must pay no attention to those maidens. Because they work in the inner ward and directly serve the nobility they think they are better than you," he said kindly while he dried her tears with gentle thumbs.

She looked up gratefully at this young handsome knight whom she knew since her early childhood. Most of the other knights of the castle ignored her; some actually found it embarrassing to look at her, lest they rudely stare. Their behavior hurt her deeply especially in her observing how very nice they were to the other children of the king's court. On the other hand, Sir Ira had always been kind to her. His brown eyes emitted warmth as though he saw in her a beautiful child or at least a normal one. Moreover, he was a close friend of the prince, her brother who loved his sister very much. For fear he would recognize her, she adjusted the wig strands over her face and hoped her large nose still obvious to a blind man would not give her away. She bowed her head and softly thanked him and added that she would dutifully return to her serf chores. She could not refrain from saying, having taken a few steps, "Thank you, Sir Ira, for protecting me."

He looked puzzled and called after her, "Odd, you serfs usually don't address us by name."

"O verily, sir, but you are an exception." She giggled and disappeared behind the kitchen building.

She heard her mother's voice; she turned from the balcony wall. The queen parted the summer curtain, which helped keep flies and mosquitos from invading the castle. She reached up and put her hands on her daughter's broad shoulders. The queen, a small comely woman, could never disguise her discomfort in being in the presence of her daughter who now dwarfed her mother. At twenty the princess in young womanhood had rid herself somewhat of her earlier gangling stature by filling out but unfortunately more to the cutting of a rather masculine figure. This not too privately upset her mother even more: reminding the queen all too vividly of the lasting feeling of having borne a child that the witches had cursed by assuming the skills of a haplessly bewitched midwife, whom later the king, to stamp out witchcraft from the land, had her summarily beheaded after having laid eyes on his frightful daughter. The queen announced coldly that

she and the king decided to hold a grand twenty-first birthday party for their daughter.

"Every important family in the kingdom, also some faraway lands, will be invited, particularly those with young sons."

The princess frowned. "Really, mother, I rather doubt that would do any good. I wish you would give up the ghost of trying to marry me off."

The queen stepped back and turned to look over the wall. She too looked down wistfully at the lovely maidens below. She thought she saw the head of the midwife laughing up at her from the bottom of the well.

"And I wish," she said, turning back to her daughter, "that you not express it in that manner. Heavens, you sound as though I were trying to get rid of you."

"Aren't you, mother?"

"I simply want you to be happy and lead a normal life," the queen patronized, looking into her daughter's sad, beady eyes.

"But I do lead a normal life — for a princess — unless you mean one out of a fairy tale."

61

"Good grief, Amanda, you know perfectly well that every respectable girl your age is married," the mother reminded her as she was wont to do whenever the subject came up.

Amanda snorted heavily. "Except for those in the nunnery... perhaps you could send me there."

The queen knitted her brows and pursed her lips, "Your sarcasm is not appreciated, especially not where your father is concerned. He hates me as it is for not bearing him *two* sons."

"Yes, and especially now that he's stuck with an ugly, unmarriageable daughter, eh? Still, mother, he should hate himself for sending his only son to war — and my only companion." Her mind was swept up by that day when her brother's steed rode into the castle ward mounted by her dead brother still in armor and tied to his mount while his bloodied knights, despondent in defeat and lamenting their leader, followed him in. She shook it off and gazed down at her mother who seemed in deep thought. "That's really what this is all about...I mean, to insure an heir to the throne....Of course, I myself must live long enough to assume the crown."

Her mother stared up at her through unblinking eyes and sputtered, "I'm not so sure that will be enough for him." She whisked her hand across her daughter's shoulder, then stepped timidly to the wall and reached out for it as though to brace herself. She looked down; this time not really seeing anything.

"Mother, heavens, what's wrong?" Amanda went over to comfort her.

"He wants me dead."

"Who?...Oh, mother, you can't be serious... surely not father," the princess tried to assure her.

"I'd be dead already had I not awakened in the night half suffocating. Your father had the pillow to my face. Apparently when I stirred he couldn't go through with it."

"Oh, no, mother! You have to be imagining it! Verily, it was but a dream, a mare."

"It was no dream. He even explained that he was tossing and turning and somehow his pillow wound up in my face! Can you imagine? Oh, what a brute of a man he is!" the queen whimpered, wringing her hands.

"Even if you're not imagining it,...why on earth would he do such a terrible thing?" Amanda dropped her large hand to her mother's tiny shoulder.

"He's quite mad, you know...." She blessed herself. "The Pope,..." the mother said with resign, "yes, to defy the Pope and God. I swear the witches have crossed his path, too."

"Too?" To help understand her babbling, Amanda tried to fathom her mother's sad but beautiful eyes, but they lowered to the floor...."Then you do..."

"Just a slip, my child, of course, I don't. You must never think that." "But Rosetta..."

"Never mind Rosetta...she naturally will never get over it and will say all sorts of things, the poor child....Oh, such an awful, awful thing for the poor dear to have to carry all her life. Oh, my child, I swear, your father, that man of divine right, is possessed!"

Amanda stretched her narrow eyes, a gasp fell from her loose lips. "Then it is the truth after all. Rosetta is not imagining it."

"It was many years I didn't believe it....And now," she sighed, "the truth now I fear is that your father is completely mad."

The princess shook her head. "Mother, get hold of yourself!" "Oh, my darling daughter, I know I've been an awful mother...yes, yes, I admit it....I couldn't accept....But I know you are beautiful within....You must help me. Perhaps if you did get married, the prospect of a grandson might be enough to erase this current notion from his sick brain."

The princess leaned over the wall; she too saw nothing. Her long

63

lumpy fingers stroked her jutting chin. She said, "There may also be the notion that he is revolted by the prospect of my being queen, in which case my marrying would do no good."

The queen reached over for her daughter's hand and pleaded, "Oh, beast that he is! Still, you cannot mean that he would still want a son!" "And why not?" Amanda countered. "Did he not want a divorce right after the battle?"

"Yes, but I thought it was that he just hated me! Or simply wanted a young one to toy with."

"Well, he does that already — and with Rosetta, the chambermaids say," Amanda said, puzzled. "He doesn't have to marry for that." The queen continued to wring her hands into a sweat and said, "Oh, my, my,…but still, Amanda, there's a chance that your marriage could change all that.…Please, my…beautiful…daughter, you will do this for me?"

The queen summoned her most trusted knight, Sir Ira. He had survived the bloody battle in which her son was killed. But he was horribly disfigured in desperately trying to save the prince who was under a wedging attack from crack warriors deep within the savage territory that adjoined the nation's southern frontier. Out of desperation the queen was completely open to Ira about her fearful relationship with the king.

With the exception of the king's attempt on her life, of which Sir Ira was skeptical but would take no chances with regard to the royal family, it was common knowledge that the king several years after the birth of his daughter had been badgering the Pope to grant him a divorce. The knight agreed to organize trusted palace guards to be on watch covering the twenty-four tumbles of the hour glass because he knew the king was capable of violence: it was open news to the nobility that the king indeed had ordered the midwife's death. There were tales, too, of other atrocities over the years of his reign.

The queen would now live in virtual isolation within her own castle apartments and whenever in the presence of the king Sir Ira would be within a sword's length. Sir Ira also decided to keep close security on the princess, thinking that the king might indeed lash out on her daughter as the first cause of the problem. The knight also made sure that the king was constantly supplied with women to keep him occupied and satisfied even though he was sure his own ex-betrothed, Rosetta, more than filled the king's desires.

When the king was informed of the queen's unexpected strategy he was infuriated, but his counselor remonstrated that it would be wise not to make an issue of it. The king abandoned his intentions toward the queen to await the outcome of the birthday ball for his daughter. Besides, he concurred with his counselor that he could no longer rely on his knights whose loyalty to him diminished in wake of his having sent them off to wage an offense against the southern foe when they were in favor — including the prince — to set up defensive positions on the frontier. Further, when he learned of Sir Ira — the most gallant and respected among the knights and court — personally championing the queen, the king's hatred for the queen was repressed out of necessity for his own survival.

Lady Rosetta was to become a very beautiful lady of the court. When the princess reached the age of sixteen, Rosetta had been assigned by the queen to be the lady-in-waiting for her daughter. The queen had hoped that this enchanting girl could somehow make her daughter presentable. Quite simply, Rosetta detested this duty because she was incapable of relating to anything or anyone ugly; moreover, she held the princess responsible for her own childhood anxiety, which often emerged when caring for her charge. Even the princess seemed to notice the hostility — though not as openly as she had shown that day long ago at the laundry spring; for she was the beautiful redhead that was so cruel to the princess. There were times when Rosetta cruelly would brush the princess' hair with undue force or when cutting it she would momentarily hold the cutting edge near Amanda's throat. Several times the princess would awaken to find Rosetta standing over her, fondling her dagger, smiling strangely.

The princess had tolerated her abusive actions — at times Rosetta could be very sweet — for in the main Rosetta's beauty tips were a big help indeed in fulfilling the queen's dictum to make her daughter at least presentable. Besides, within the last two years Rosetta curiously seemed kinder and gentler.

Before the great defeat to the south, Rosetta was madly in love with Ira, and they were betroth. After his return from battle and the surgeon had removed the bandages from his face, she could not bear to look upon him. She avoided him for months after that; subsequently Ira released her from their commitment. Upon learning of this the princess was shocked and summarily dismissed Rosetta from her position — to the delight of Rosetta who then began to take up flirtations with the king, prompting him to renew his quest for a divorce.

Though the king was not handsome, Rosetta found him attractive because he was tall and still had the build of a muscular young man, making her ultimate plan, brewing for some time, tolerable. For, aside from Ira's once handsome face, his strong physique had attracted her as well since torrid physical love was paramount to her. In fact, it would have been possible in time had the scars on Ira's face waned, she could accept him at least for impassioned love-making; however, in addition to the deep disfigurement, he had permanently lost the use of his left arm, horribly mangled and shriveled, which was too much for her to bear.

She was not totally shallow, however, for when the princess had dismissed her, and though she never wanted the assignment in the first place, she was ashamed for not having the courage to remain with Ira for whom she still possessed sympathy and respect. Furthermore, by not marrying Ira, she perhaps lost the opportunity to manipulate him in order to carry out her plan that had forged in her mind when she first learned of its cause two years ago. More than a year had lapsed since the great battle, but Rosetta could not muster the courage to carry out her plan alone. Recent complications, however, altered her plan, and she reasoned that what she intended to do now would be far more devastating and to her satisfying.

In deference to the queen, who had enjoyed a close relationship with the maiden's mother, Rosetta agreed to prepare the princess for the ball. In private audience with the queen, she said, "Your highness, of late I have taken a new look at the princess. There is a charm about her that I am sure I can exhibit in her countenance at the ball." "Oh?...And pray, why the sudden change?" the queen quizzed, taken by surprise; for it was no mystery to her of Rosetta's dislike for her daughter.

"Not sudden, your highness, attitudes seldom are." "Then the charm has always been there, eh? And it took time for you to see it."

"I suppose, you could say that,...yes," she admitted, lowering her eyes.

"Beauty, then, is in the beholder, eh?" The queen chuckled. Rosetta laughed, revealing beautiful teeth. The queen too had all her teeth, which were reasonably straight and bright; but she was always envious of this maiden's, which in contrast brought to mind the awful jagged teeth of Amanda's.

"Possibly, my lady," Rosetta said after giving it some thought, "yet the source has to have some merit — surely the princess has that." She could not refrain from thinking of Ira. She wondered if

67

she could have matured equally with respect to him and love again. But Rosetta knew the difference; for she would always love him, but never again as intimate lovers. She thought again, "Of course, I suppose, there has to be some merit in the beholder as well, else she is sure to miss something."

Solemnly the queen said, "You know, Rosetta, your mother saw beauty in everything....Yes, she comforted me during the birth of Amanda, who to your mother was a beautiful baby."

Rosetta looked to the flagstone floor for a moment. "Too bad she could not convince the king of that."

The queen blurted, "Oh, such a waste, such a meaningless sacrifice!" She bowed her head and cleared her voice. "In truth, so tragically true!...For years I could not force myself to believe that story. I believed my husband."

"Oh, my queen! How could you have thought that of my mother! You knew her so well!"

"I know, my child, it was so very wrong of me. It was young pride, selfishness, to think witchcraft was behind it. I just couldn't address the thought that I could bear such a child without the intervention of a witch even though deep down inside I knew that your mother could never have been one, nor susceptible of one's spell."

"But why didn't you intervene on her behalf?" she asked in a pleading, strained voice as she had asked herself a thousand times.

"Oh, my darling child, surely you didn't think all these years that I had anything to do with it! Three months had gone by before I suspected. I had been told that your mother had gone to visit your grandmother." The queen began to tug on her jeweled ring while thinking of her long lost friend.

Again Rosetta cast her green eyes, lacking their customary lustre, to the flagstones. "I never knew the cause of her death until a few years ago after I returned from the north. As you know, my father had sent me away to be raised by my grandmother and apparently to protect me from the real cause." Rosetta bowed before her and took the queen's ringed hand and kissed it. "No, I never really believed that you would not have rushed to her aid in her hour of need if you could. Still, it is comforting to hear it from you." The queen leaned over and urged the tearful maiden's head in her lap and stroked her light red hair while they traded sobs.

Later, the princess swallowed her pride and welcomed Rosetta with a series of hugs, then excitedly she said, "I welcome you back, Rosetta, not as a miracle-worker, but as a friend. There is little you can do with the likes of me, except lift my spirits as I fear this coming ball."   "Oh, but you shouldn't, your highness, you will be a shining star, trust me."

"You mean more like Mars — thanks to my imposing red nose!" The princess with her finger and thumb wiggled her nose vigorously till it turned red and laughed.

Rosetta laughed too, but then took on a serious air and said, "Powder works wonders."

"You'll need a ton!" And they both laughed merrily. Just then a maiden, Rosetta's replacement, since her dismissal, entered to inform the princess that Sir Ira requested an audience. The princess' dark squinty eyes widened and sparkled. She hurried the maiden out to retrieve him. Rosetta's delicate chin quivered, then said that she would leave by another door. "No, dear lady, you must not be rude," the princess chided.

"In that respect, I'm afraid I have already won honors," Rosetta said sadly.

"True, and for that I shan't ever forgive you treating such a wonderful man as you did shamelessly. Still, you must remain friends. I insist."

"Oh, I should very much like that; but I fear he..."

69

"Shush, none of that. Ira is all forgiving. It is his nature to be nice to everyone." She squinted and then chuckled. "Yes, even to you, my dear."

Upon entering, he momentarily froze in his tracks in seeing his beautiful ex-fiancée; then he approached the princess, bowed to kiss her hand and with conscious effort kept the scar-free side of his face to Rosetta, who noticed that he no longer wore a half mask. Only the eye socket was patched. She did not know that the princess insist that he not wear one in her presence because she was proud of his emblem of courage in battle. Nervously he cleared his throat several times and finally addressed the princess, "I do not wish to alarm you, your highness. But it has been rumored that the enemy from the south might try to invade the castle during the ball. Because of this I cannot attend and insist that you and the queen be careful, even though I am leaving Sir Seth by your side."

"Oh, but I am alarmed, not for my mother nor myself, but for you. What is it you intend to do?"

"Most of us knights are going to command a line of defense by Green Ridge pass to keep the southern rabble away from the castle. Frankly, I do not expect them to be so foolish, but to be on the safe side we must engage this maneuver," he said commandingly.

Rather than stand there in silence and stare at his beautiful side, Rosetta rejoined, "Ira, what could this possibly mean? Why, the savages below have never penetrated this far up from the frontier?"

Careful not to turn his scarred side to her he choked out, "Th-that's true R...my lady, but their resounding victory last year might have given them mad confidence."

Rosetta gazed into the same, beautiful warm blue eye as she had done many times when he had both. A shivering feeling came over her — without the complement of the other it was not the same. He shuddered too from the thought that this beautiful image that

70

had once been his possession was now the mistress of the king. Virtually lost in her presence he was grateful that the princess broke the pause.

"I trust, Ira, it is truly maddening and there is no merit to their confidence?" She stared right into his gnarled profile.

"Verily, princess, their victory came at a high price," he attested, casting his eye from Rosetta, almost reluctantly.

"Yes, war is costly, win or lose." Her brother flashed in her mind. "Ira, would it not be wise for us to cancel the ball? Really, it is so unnecessary — and surely it will not realize my mother's purpose."

"My dear princess," Rosetta interspersed, "purpose or not, it is tradition to celebrate the coming of age. Did we not both enjoy your brother's?"

"Indeed, and to cancel on rumor," said Ira, "would be giving in to the enemy."

"Oh, but stout knight," the princess wailed, "why must you...and our gallant men be sent from the protection of the castle? Surely, they cannot penetrate our walls!"

"Too great a risk, your highness. We are not sure of their strength. They could conceivably hold us under siege, like the hunter's dogs caught in his master's traps. Nay, better that we take the vantage point."

"Then God be with you and your gallant band," the princess said solemnly.

Ira had been sent for early in the morning to the king's bedroom to rattle him. Rosetta was still in bed with the king. The king feared that Ira had lost the nerve for war and that this would seethe him sufficiently to regain the knight's prowess. The king had always believed that his knights had failed him in the battle owing to his son's objections in attacking the southern foe in the first place. It worked for the wrong reason — Ira needed no motivation where

71

the savages were concerned. Ira's temper boiled but served only to solidify his union with the queen. Rosetta was clearly embarrassed, momentarily pulling the covers over her head. When she lowered them and looked over at Ira, who deliberately turned his disfigured side to her, she jerked down the covers, revealing her sumptuous nude body. She looked over at the king's side with anger in her heart and screeched, "There, my king, now your strategy is complete."

Ira cast his eye to her and saw that she was pregnant. Abruptly he turned to the king; the knuckles of his good right hand turned white as he gripped the hilt. His eye blazed. The king now standing on the platform edge froze momentarily in terror, but when Ira turned his back to them, the king relaxed, stepped off the platform and said, recapturing his composure, "Ira, I simply wanted you to know that your decision to meet the enemy at Green Ridge is sound; however, I must insist that should the enemy appear undermanned that you go on the offensive and rout them as you should have the last time."

Ira swung back on his boot heels and snarled. "What sort of king are you? Surely, divine-right has gone awry in your case!"

The king grunted. "How dare you!"

"How dare *you*!" Ira just as bluntly corrected him. "You who sent your son and hundreds of others to their death dare speak to me of this! Kiss good lady fortune that I am an honorable knight or I swear I'd strike you down this instant!"

The king hesitantly, placed his hand fawningly on Ira's shoulder. Ira backed away. "Now, now, Ira, I know that you are unquestionably the finest and loyal," he said obsequiously, turning on his heel to get a glimpse of Rosetta, who had the coverlet to her eyes. He faced the knight again and regained a commanding tone. "I shall overlook your remarks…and truly admit that it is, after all, your command

and you will do what has to be done."

"Then why summon me here in the first place? I shall take my leave and leave you to your pleasure." He scowled over at Rosetta. She jumped out of the bed as he turned to leave. Quickly she donned a robe and ran after him, dropping to her knees and wrapping her arms about his thighs. He stopped at the doorway. She reached for and squeezed his shriveled hand. He felt her hot tears flowing into the scars.

"Oh, my darling, my sweet, darling Ira, please, please forgive me... forgive me!...Oh, I know it is so much to ask....Yet I beg you!...If not from you, then Christ Himself cannot!" She drowned his ugly hand in wet kisses.

He raised her up, drew her close momentarily with his good arm. Then caressed her hair, beautifully rich in the early morning light. He lifted her chin and said, "Take a good, close look and you will see there is nothing that I can forgive you for."

"Oh, no, my dear, I was terribly wrong!"

"No, Rosetta, it is in your nature. There was nothing you could do about it. Besides, I would never have allowed you to go on loving me. I should die first."

"Oh, my sweet, I'll change my nature!"

"No, it is too late for that." He rubbed her protuberant stomach, then released her and started for the exit.

She fell to the floor, weeping. The king went to her and lifted her to the bed, saying, "A disgusting display of conscience, my dear — I had no idea you had one."

She looked up with a frown. "I had no idea you could recognize one who had."

Several days before the ball Ira positioned the knights and foot soldiers on the north side of Green Ridge. The canard was indeed true; messengers reported that the enemy had crossed the border marauding villages and was heading this way. Early the next morning the king's men were on the alert while in silence they watched at the break of dawn the barbaric state stealthily moving its forces toward the kingdom's first and only true line of defense. Ira and the knights kept the royal forces calm, ensconced behind the ridge edge until the savages came within crossbow range. When the enemy, suspecting there might be resistance at the mountain, rose up to charge, hundreds of arrows greeted them. The enemy, although geared with breast plate and shield, fell by the droves as Ira ordered that the bowman aim for bare arms and legs.

Nevertheless scores of the enemy negotiated half way up the ridge. Ira mounted his great steed and signaled the other knights to follow him along a trail that swept round the ridge into heavy brush high on the other side where they had relative safety to line up abreast ready to counterattack. When Ira raised his lance and spurred his horse the others jumped to a quick gait and they swarmed down on the vanguard of the enemy. With their lances and swords, quickly and deftly the knights slew the disorganized intruders unqualified to meet head on the superbly trained knights.

Subsequently Ira signaled the captain of the other horsemen and foot-soldiers to advance down the side. The horsemen lined up abreast with the knights. Ira checked to see that the foot soldiers were ready to follow. He handed his lance to one of the horseman next to him, raised his sword and called them to battle. Loping through the foothills and onto the plain, the steeds steadily quickened their gate. Ira, however, set the pace to be sure the foot soldiers were not left too far behind, though they were running at a rapid rate. The knights pulled ahead of the regular royal cavalry and formed a wedge with Ira at the point. They broke through the enemy line on foot and aimed straight for the warlord's crack guards and

74

engaged them in heavy combat while the other horsemen and foot soldiers circled the front line and closed in for the kill. From the shadows of early dawn into the bright sun of mid morning fierce, blood-splattering conflict raged. The vengeful knights in particular did not abide by and chivalric code of battle, so determined were they to conquer without mercy in honor of their dead prince.

Near the end of the battle Ira was ripped from his horse after being under attack by four guards, all of whom fell to his might, but the robust warlord himself charged Ira from behind with a menacing blow of his mace. The wooly warlord dismounted and was about to bash in Ira's skull when a heavily armored foot soldier rushed to Ira's defense with a powerful swoop of a sword across the mace handle, then a quick blow to the warlord's head. The warlord fell back on his haunches. Coughing blood onto his wide beard, compounded by an earlier wound in the fray, he moaned, "And I thought your king had lost control." "You might be right about our king; but the kingdom is still in control," the foot soldier muttered through the visor. The warlord's head jerked back, his eyes glazed and his scrubby bearded jaw dropped. He died on his knees before toppling over.

As the knights formed an enclave about the wounded Ira, the foot soldier kneeled beside Ira and applied a bandage to the cutting wound on his good side. The smashing blow had fragmented the visor hinge, which cut deeply into the vestige of his handsome face. Nevertheless, he managed a smile when told hostilities ended as soon as the gritty remnants saw their lord master spat out his bloody life for the last time.

A grateful Ira extended his arm to reach for the soldier's visor. "I must see the face of the friend who saved my life."

The soldier calmly continued bandaging him. Ira flicked open the visor. Amanda smiled down at him.

75

While a few knights and a small band of horse and foot soldiers escorted the enemy's captured and wounded over the border, Ira was delivered to the castle apothecary-hospital with his fellow wounded. The small building, maintained by hospitallers and the castle physician, who had just entered to confer with the nuns. He then personally checked on each of the other wounded before approaching Ira, who was anxious to be released. The doctor carefully lifted one end of the bandage to examine the cheek wound. He squinted and said, "Good, the swelling is not from an infection but from the fractured cheek bone."

"Fine, then I'm out of here. " Ira sat up straight, then reeled and lay back down from faintness.

"Don't be so anxious, good sir, you still have some concussion; besides, you have a badly sprained ankle from catching the foot in the stirrup when the shaggy savage assailed you."

"But the princess' ball!"

"Oh, that's been canceled — over the king's protest, I should add;... it seems the princess would have no celebration while so many lie here wounded. She says when there is a ball it will not be to honor her but rather for the men who brought us glorious victory over the uncivilized."

"Ah, yes, that's she, all right. Always the beautiful angel." "Beautiful?...Why, yes," the physician reflected, "I suppose, she is...where it truly matters." His weary eyes widened from insight, adding definitively, "Yes, verily."

Ira smiled at a nun tending to him. "Since a child she has shown that...intangible beauty — what does the cover matter? Look at me, definitely not the same man of a few years back, nay, a better man, I think." The modest knight's words surprised himself as he stared over at the physician.

"That you are,... a national hero," the nun inserted.

"Oh, I don't mean it that way. Ever since I was disfigured I've turned more into myself." Ira raised the patch to wipe away beads of sweat. "The exterior never really allowed me to get to know myself." "My, a mighty warrior that now speaks in oracles, too," the physician jibed. "I'd better let up on your medication."

"The princess, I think, always had that advantage of being at peace with herself. Oh, she will make a grand monarch someday!" "Oh?...I doubt she will have the chance," remarked the physician, quickly changing his expression.

"What! Nay! What are you saying?" Having sat up abruptly, Ira pressed his good hand to his head.

The physician applied a cold pack to the knight's forehead. He cautioned, "You must not excite yourself. You've had a blow that could have felled a moose!...The king, you know, is bent on having a replacement for his son. In examining Rosetta, I'm sure that he will have one....And even if not, he'll try with her again."

"But surely, you don't mean he would usurp primogeniture for the sake of a bastardy son!"

"Oh, pope or no pope, queen or no queen, he is determined to marry again!"

Ira let his head back onto the pillow and sighed. "It's insane. How could he do this to his own flesh and blood?"

"Well, Rosetta's will be his too, you know?"

"Aye, but it is not the same, is it?...Why, it goes against God's ways." Ira glanced at the nun who made the sign of the cross and nodded.

"Ah, but not against the king's ways!" the doctor reminded Ira and the nun.

"Aye, the way of madness. Thank God they are under guard." Ira let out a sigh.

"Who?"

77

"Why, the queen and the princess."

Later the same day, the princess visited the wounded along with her train of beautiful handmaidens, including Rosetta who had recruited them on behalf of the princess. They all bore gifts to lift the spirits of their heroes. While the maidens talked and joked with the warriors, the princess and Rosetta went over to Ira who was sound asleep. They talked softly over him. "Oh, my," Rosetta whispered, "now his other side?...Why, you never told me, Amanda."

"I told you he was badly wounded, didn't I? You never inquired further,"the princess said in a soft, but firm tone. "Besides, why should it matter? The important thing is that he still has the use of one hand. And once the ankle is sound again, he'll be up and about as good as new."

"Oh, I know," Rosetta intoned apologetically; "still, such a handsome face..."

"Rosetta, shame! I thought you were getting over your obsession with appearances." The princess in rebuking her slapped Rosetta's hand.

"Oh, forgive, me, your highness, I'm incorrigible...Of course, he's alive that's all that matters," she agreed, rubbing her hand.

"Exactly, and the nation has been spared the loss of another great leader," the princess said sadly while looking down at him warmly.

Rosetta as if in contrition flickered her beautiful eyes at the princess. "And you, my dear Amanda,...have you too been spared?"

The king was furious with the princess for refusing to go through with the ball for which he had arranged several suitors from foreign lands to choose her for a hefty dowry. He had reasoned that with her out of the kingdom for a spell his ultimate plan would be far less complicated. Now, however, when Rosetta informed him of a possible romantic linkage between the princess and Ira, his hopes were dashed. Wine and a restless night — what with Rosetta's rejecting him since she learned of her pregnancy and her behavior with Ira right under his nose in this very room — he rose up before dawn, several hours before his accustomed awakening. Instead of relaxing him the heavy wine stirred the wildness in his mind. Quietly he strapped on his sword belt over his night gown and threw on his morning robe. In his bare feet he stepped into the cold interior stairwell linking his room to the queen's below.

To his surprise, as he twisted down the steps, he saw a guard sitting on one of the steps. He was slumped over. Uncertain that he was asleep, the king slowly drew his sword with both hands, lifting it high, and plunged it into the back of the guard's neck. The guard gurgled, recoiled, then leaned further forward; the king grabbed him and pushed him back against the steps, lest the noise of the fall draw attention. The king continued down the steps to a door leading to a room adjacent to the queen's inner bedroom. He pushed gently against the door, but it still creaked.

Sir Seth, ever alert, bounced from the queen's apartment vestibule. Quickly he lit a candle and accosted the shadowy figure that was slowly approaching the queen's inner door. In the flickering light, he said, "Don't do this, my lord. I do not wish to be party to regicide either way. But I have my orders from Ira."

"Bah, all this talk of Ira," the king grunted. "Why, people are saying *he* is the king!" Nodding absently and rubbing his nose alternately with stroking his closely cropped beard, he squinted up at the knight and clacked, shaking a finger at him. "I now firmly believe — aye, aye — those canards that he had my son killed on the battlefield to make himself king."

Seth laughed. "Only the devil could think that of Ira. I fear you've had too much wine last night, your majesty. I suggest you return to

79

your bed and sleep away the day. It will give you a clearer perspective on the truth. For, your presence here at this hour smells of trouble I would rather you avoid."

"You young knights — no longer loyal to the crown — only to yourselves!"

"Our loyalty, my king, is to the entire royal family, not just the king."

"Exactly the attitude of you snip-snaps: glibly phrase it, will you? — not just the king." Then he nodded his head emphatically, and changing his tone with a yawn, he said while walking past him to the outermost room, "Yea, you're probably right — it is the wine." Seth smiled and paced behind him a few steps, then veered to place the candle on a table. With lightning speed the king withdrew his sword and thrust it into Seth's back. Seth slumped while struggling to grip the hilt of his own sword. The king cruelly twisted his bloody sword in drawing it back out. Seth howled in pain, and dropped to the cold slabs.

Meanwhile Rosetta had wakened and seeing that the king was not by her side, she flung back the coverlet and quickly donned her robe. Noting the interior door was ajar, she went down the winding stairs. She gasped at the sight of the dead guard and froze momentarily, pressing her palms onto her womb. Then she eased by the body and continued her descent to the queen's room. She could hear the king's angry, muffled voice in the queen's bedroom. Dawn's gray forelight peeped through the outer window of the vestibule dimly lighting the arch. She went under it. She wondered why Seth had not intervened. She shrilled in seeing him face down on the cold slabs. She kneeled next to him and sobbed as the blood still oozed from his mouth. Taking a deep breath to stop her sobs, she unlocked his hand from the hilt, removing the sword. Then cautiously, sword by her side, she went toward the queen's bedroom.

"One last time," the king one knee in the bed, said menacingly, "divorce or death."

"How dare you speak to me of such blasphemy," said the queen, sitting up in bed bravely, "Oh, I always knew you were capable of such treachery; yet somehow I pretended that you were just a blathering idiot. I ask you now, my king, that you return to your room and sleep off this hellish mood. I've begged you oft-times to swear off the heavy wine."

The king's eyes flared as he raised his bloody sword for a moment then lowered it. "It is not wine but the curséd blood you brought to my royal line."

She gasped at the sight of the sword dripping with blood; she cowered. "My God, what have you done? Pray, not our dear Amanda!" "There are other means of dealing with her, my wife — *wife*!" he repeated, "what a joke." He laughed cruelly. "Better had you been barren."

She knitted her brows and stared at him venomously, then looked down at the blood. "How did you get in here? Where is Seth?...Oh, no," she gasped. "You didn't,...you couldn't!"

"Couldn't, eh? Just as I couldn't..." He raised the sword again. "Grant me the divorce or I shall take my freedom in blood."

"Never!" She shrilled. "Amanda is divinely destined to be monarch!" She tried to scramble out of the bed, but he restricted her with a partial thrust of his sword. She cringed and lay back into the pillows.

"I take it this is your final answer?"

"It is!" she said defiantly, crossing her arms. "Though I go to my death, the people and our moral knights will run you into damnation."

"Then damnation to you! For death it is!" His arm sprung back

81

for the thrust.

"Indeed!" screamed Rosetta who ran with Seth's sword and plunged it into the king's back and out the chest. The queen screamed and turned into the pillow.

The king rattled and slumped forward; his torso jack-knifed over the edge of the bed, pulling the bed drapery with him. Gasping, he moaned into the canopy over his head, "Bitch of a bastardy child!...I'll see you in hell, my whore."

Rosetta wailed hideously. "Bloody executioner of a midwife!...I'll see you there sooner than you think." Midst the queen's sobs into the pillow, she jumped off the bed, yanked out the sword, spun his body face up and stuck the sword into him again, but the king was already dead. "What a pity, you could not suffer the last thrust and hear the dying doomsday voice of a tyrant!" She glanced over at the queen who was still turned into the pillow. She glared down at the body again. "Still, my revenge is sweet even though I now must join you in the devil's fiery pit." The queen rose from the security of the pillow and with horror looked over at this avenging angel. Rosetta released the hilt; the bloody blade swayed in the throat's gurgling after death. Rosetta said to the horrified queen. "Dear highness, forgive me,...and please, be so kind too to ask Amanda and Ira to forgive a shallow fool!" She ran to the window and jumped onto its wide ledge.

"No, Rosetta!" the queen screeched. "The kingdom forgives you!" She looked up to the pinkish sky. "May my God and my son forgive me, too!" Her hands to her womb, she leaped to her death.

A month later a great threefold national celebration was held in the kingdom. Finally a great ball was held at the castle in behalf of the victorious army, the coronation of Queen Amanda; and to consummate the glorious day at the altar the queen monarch looking up at Ira's beautiful side of a face, the swelling gone, was asked the solemn vow by the celebrant priest, to which the new queen and bride, stressed, "Oh, yea, father, I *do verily* and with all the strength and beauty I feel this day in my heart."

And an incandescence fired in from the chapel window and lighted on the happy couple. All present marveled at the glowing warmth of his good side, and her beautiful long silky waves cascading rivulets of starry magic.

Sun & Wind Rematch

March Wind was feeling rather chipper this morning, stirring up a storm here and there, but mostly puffing out annoying gusts. Grownups along the streets on their way to work or shopping struggling under his might, he enjoyed. His favorite time of day was between eight and nine in the morning and again at between three and four in the afternoon: school children was his favorite pastime because they weren't as strong. He would laugh uproariously between mighty puffs when he saw homework papers flying from a hand or a hat lift suddenly from a head. He laughed so hard at a little girl with a red schoolbag running after her Brownie cap, while trying desperately to keep her long hair from flapping her eyes, that he had to rest. It disappointed him that the girl was now free to regain her cap and that he would not be able to blow away her schoolbag; but he was determined to seek her out after school.

He rolled back further up into the sky to visit his uncle, the sun, who was lying behind a cloud. Because of his age old Sol decided that spring could wait awhile longer and let his prankster nephew Gusty March enjoy himself. Ever since the time some hundred years ago when Gusty playfully challenged him to a match but lost, Uncle Sol had felt sorry for Gusty and pretty much let him have his way — though Gusty was careful to reasonably behave himself when Sol was looking. Today, because Gusty was feeling so powerful since he was

well-rested from early rains working so hard for the last week, he decided he would once again challenge old Sol.

When he approached dosing Sol, he had to puff away his uncle's hot breath passing through his heavy snores. When Sol stopped snoring, Gusty quickly blew cold breezes into his ruddy face. Sol jerked open his red eyes and groaned, "Oh, it's you, is it?...Up to mischief again, eh? You take an awful chance sneaking up on me like that. My solar winds could burn you out completely — they don't like competition from upstarts, you know."

"Good heavens, Uncle Sol, have you no sense of humor?" he asked nervously, knowing Sol's hot temper. "You did in the old days. Remember when you tricked me long ago?...And didn't I take it like a sport?"

"His gas burped deep within. "What do you mean tricked you. It was a fair contest."

"In the result only. I meant that in the contest you had to remove that man's cloak. He removed it himself!"

"True, but he never would have if I hadn't sweated it off him," Sol reminded him. "And you couldn't expect me to burn it off him."

"Just the same you tricked me," Gusty whined.

"Well, so did the man. After all, he was too smart and strong for you. And you used no strategy as I had."

"Sure, people expect me in March; they don't expect ninety degrees in my season. I tell you it was an unfair contest. You could never have gotten away with it against my cousin Hurricane."

"So you want a rematch with my other nephew to do battle for you — can't blow your own wind, eh?"

"Hold on, Uncle Sol, you're cooking too fast! I do want a rematch, but I've got plenty of wind to take care of it myself," Gusty said with a huff and a puff.

"It's okay by me — either way you lose. I can boil away the force of both of you," Sol boasted, flapping his flames with pride.

"Don't be so sure of yourself. Don't forget I was confident the last time, too — and I lost."

Old Sol tilted his axis and belched out a gaseous flame and laughed. "You sure were cocky; perhaps I shouldn't have taught you a lesson. Elders should, after all, let the young ones win once in a while. Well, what's the challenge this time? But I warn you, nowadays they wear coats and not cloaks which will make it all the harder for your tired lungs to heave up enough force to blow off."

"Oh, that isn't the deal now — too smart for that," Old Gusty said. "No, this time it's going to be a little girl."

"A little girl! Gosh, Gusty, don't you have any pride?" Old Sol said angrily. "I don't want to pick on a defenseless little girl."

"Oh, don't worry; it's harmless," Gusty assured him. "All you have to do is remove her hat from her head and make her drop her schoolbag."

"You call that a challenge?" Sol chuckled out a jittery flame. "Why, when she starts to feel my rays she'll have to take off her hat and put down the schoolbag in order to rest from the heat wave. That's easy." "Yeah? We'll see. I'll meet you by that school down there at three o'clock," Gusty said blowing himself away to visit some clouds down below.

"Wait a minute — talking about dirty tricks — I'm not myself

85

this time of season, especially at that hour." Sol said, churning his solar wind.

"That's the deal. What's the matter? Can't handle it? Want to give up?" Gusty howled.

"No way do I ever concede to anything! — except my loss of bedtime, of course....Darn! I haven't had a wink since those doggone sailors proved the world was round....But you can be sure, laddy, I'll be there and whip you badly — again. Now, it would be a different story if it were my dear sweet niece, Breezy, who wafts gentle summer breezes across our earthlings, I would let her win."

At three o'clock Old Sol lowered down and angled in at the school. Some hot beads of moisture bubbled over his brows when he realized he could not ray down on the school at this hour because a tall building was in his way. He mumbled to himself, "Young Gusty has gotten wiser, but with a little sweat and bending round that building, I'll manage."

Gusty swept in right over the school. He looked up and winked at some clouds that floated above him. He controlled himself while the children rushed out into a still afternoon. When he spotted the little girl with the Brownie cap and the red schoolbag, he very softly blew high and away toward Sol so he could point her out to him. "There, below, that little girl swinging the red schoolbag! I'll go first just like the last time."

"Be my guest, but I can tell she doesn't trust you the way she's hanging on to her hat," Sol said.

Gusty blew back over; then with a sudden drop toward her he exhaled mightily, catching her off guard and she toppled over on her knees and dropped the schoolbag and the latch broke spilling some books out. To his surprise her hat stayed on! He puffed and puffed. Still the hat stayed on. He swept down right above her, but she grabbed the now badly scuffed schoolbag and held it tight over her head. Gusty was exhausted and had to let up. The girl stood up and started running. He followed until he saw that she out-foxed him by sticking a hat pin in her hair. "Oh, no," he puffed. "Oh, well, at least I got her to drop the schoolbag. He blew back up to Sol and signaled that it was his turn and added, "I can still win if you can't remove either one."

"No sweat,...come to think of it, a little sweat will do it!" Sol chuckled. He rolled down his bulk and aimed in on the little girl, who was already warm from running. She stopped to open her coat, but to Sol's surprise she didn't try to remove the coat and kept her schoolbag in her hand. She continued on to the end of the street where she turned behind the tall building and into the shade. Sol belched, "Drats!" But then a big fiery smile expanded even more his huge face when she emerged from the shade. He burned down on her with all his might. The girls' brisk pace, came to a halt and she wiped her forehead. "Ah, I've got her now!" Sol cried out. "She's ready to put down the schoolbag and remove the hat."

Instead, she brought the bag up to her body and cradled it in one arm while she raised her hand to remove the pin from the hat. Sly Gusty hiding behind a black cloud blew on it gently. The cloud floated over the girl and showered her with rain drops. She left her hat on to protect her hair and started to run, dropping her pin. Sol and the cloud followed. Sol was yelling at the cloud to get out of the way. But his nephew just kept blowing the cloud along. Old Sol, not used to working so hard this time of year had to give up but not before he spit out in angry defeat a weak solar wind to his March Wind contestant who deftly escaped the hot vacuum. Disappointed Sol continued west to get ready for sunset.

Though he already won, Gusty for good measure blew off the little's girl's brownie cap. She chased after it; and when it rolled into a puddle she cried. His proud feeling in getting even with Sol for the humiliating defeat over a hundred years ago, turned to shame as he felt sorry for the little girl. He blew away the black cloud. He then hurried to find Breezy who then quickly caught up with the little girl to take her home with gentle breezes to dry her off and her cap.

The next morning the little girl came out of the house to head for school. This time she had two hat pins. She stood on the porch to check the weather. There was an overcast — Sol was sulking behind a cloud — and there was no wind. Because her father could not fix the schoolbag, she had to carry her homework and books in an embarrassing shopping bag. As she stepped off the porch the wind stirred. "Oh, no, not again!" she cried. She held her hat and drew the bag close to her and started walking down the path when suddenly the wind dropped in front of her feet a new, shiny red schoolbag.

The Island Prince

In a remote kingdom many centuries ago there was a young prince who felt the need to govern ever since his early childhood when he would play the game ruler of the realm with the court's playmates. However, this kingdom was already well governed by his father the king.

On his sixteenth birthday the king asked his son what he wanted for his birthday. The lad did not have to think about it and immediately replied, "A princedom, my father, for I wish to govern."

The king laughed. He grasped the arms of his throne and leaned forward. He looked into his son's eyes and saw that he was serious. Said the king to the prince, "You will have enough of governing when I die. I trust you do not wish me dead already."

"Horrors, father, no, I wish you to live to be a hundred and if you reach that, then fifty more!"

The king was satisfied that his son's voice rang true: proud he was that he raised a prince ready to accept responsibility of royalty. He had heard of other kingdoms that had royal sons who wanted only to ride off and fetch a princess or simply have a frivolous time in the villages carousing and reveling in idleness. He stroked his beard and pondered for a moment. "Well, my son, there is no principality, but I suppose I could dispatch you to the southern coast where you could oversee the summer castle. How does that suit you?"

The prince shook his head demonstrably and said, "Oh, forgive me, my king, but that would never do."

Exasperated and with a frown on his face the king slumped in his throne. "Pray, why not? There is much to supervise — the servants at the castle, the royal guards, the village square and hundreds of serfs in the fields."

"All that is already tended to by your baronet. No, my father, I wish to govern and make laws."

"But that too we already have," the king reminded him, then cupped his hand over his mouth to hide his grin.

"On the island off the northern coast there is no government," the prince retorted.

The king laughed, then said, "There is no need for government there — the island is uninhabited."

89

"True, but why is that?" the prince pursued.

"The climate is too harsh and the soil barren," with authority said the king as he sat up straight in his throne.

"Perhaps, but there are thriving kingdoms further north with harsher climates," the prince said with confidence.

"Ah, but their soil is not barren, and their lands are plenty. Why, our island is but a grain of icy sand on the ocean's surface," said the king. He rose from the throne and descended the steps to add, "Come now, surely there is another gift I can give you on your birthday." The king put his arm around his son's shoulder and was amazed that he had to reach up. "My, you have grown so! I had no idea you were taller than I." He chuckled with pride. "Perhaps I should abdicate and give the crown to you."

The prince smiled and responded, "Do not jest, father; I know that I am not ready for that. That is why I want to apprentice in governance and thus to learn."

"Then I shall make you my chancellor's assistant. A brilliant man as he could teach you much about government."

"No, father, there's time for that. Right now, I request that you grant me the challenge to govern the island."

He laughed and rocked the boy's shoulder. "Why, you would be bored to death as a recluse— unless you take half the royal library with you!"

"No, my king, I intend to take people with me," the prince said with assurance.

"My boy, you are serious! It seems you have given this some thought. And just how do you propose to do that? Who would go with you to such a barren land?"

The prince did not have to think over the question. "I was hoping you would have the royal knights round up the beggars, the invalids and the homeless and put them aboard your merchant ship."

The king's eyes popped, astonished that this young son of his seemed to have an answer for everything. "Oh, why not the thieves in the stockades as well?" he said with a grin.

"Of course, why didn't I think of that? Yes, yes, that would make even more urgent the need to legislate," the young prince said with enthusiasm.

The king in deep thought, scratched his beard and offered, "And why didn't I think of that? Why, it is a marvelous idea to rid our city of worthless baggage. And why didn't my chancellor think of it to cleanse our city? Aye, I shall have him work on this at once."

"Oh, thank you, father, for this wonderful birthday gift!" his son squealed excitedly.

His father looked at him with curiosity. "Eh?...Oh, my goodness, no!...I did not mean that you would go. What kind of father and king do you think I am to exile you with trash? Oh, no,...why can't you be normal and wish for a prize horse or reside with the friars at the university and study law?"

"Have you forgotten, father? I have already studied under the learnéd friars. It is time to put my learning into action."

"Oh, my, that's right — how time flows. Well, a horse, then."

"Oh, father, you are jousting with me again — I already have two of the finest steeds in the kingdom." He chuckled, then looked searchingly into his father's eyes. "I must do this, my king."

The king looked away, but he still felt those soft pleading eyes on him — the queen's eyes, he thought. He returned the look and said, "Ah, you are like your dear mother — may she rest in peace. She too had persuasive powers." He smiled at him and said, "All right, my son, herewith the island is a princedom. Govern well."

The next day the king ordered his knights to scour the town for beggars, the homeless and invalids unable to work. They roped

91

together many thieves from the stockades as well, but the king warned that there should be no murderers among them. Then all — a hundred men, women and children — were herded together and placed aboard the ship where the prince was waiting.

The prince with a gracious smile upon his face, came out of his cabin on the quarterdeck and addressed the confused and frightened crowd. "Do not be alarmed, my subjects. This is a time to rejoice, for we are bound for the uninhabited island that is now called 'Promise.'"

A thin, and drawn woman in tattered clothes stepped forward from the crowd on the main-deck. She bowed before the prince and cried, "Oh, our dear prince, how can it be Promise when we are flocked together like sheep to graze upon a barren land? Though most of us are homeless, many of us find food and shelter in the church."

A powerful man in a torn shirt came forward, dragging with him his fellow thieves tied to him. Unwilling to bow, he stood defiantly before the prince, then turned to the frightened woman and scoffed, "Bah, woman, dry your eyes. At least you are not linked together with the rest like a team of oxen as we are." He turned back to the prince and added, "I'll wager your father the king no longer wants to feed us thieves at the stockades and you plan to throw us overboard or work us till we fall dead. And if the latter then I'd rather you drown us now. There is no honor among thieves if we are put to work!" The men tied to him, all nodded and grumbled.

Vexed the prince frowned, then paced awhile. His heavy boots pounded the deck as the people's hearts pounded with them. He stopped and swung on his heels and said to the thief, "Speak not of drowning, man. Such an inference is unwarranted in light of your kindly king's rule. Why, in other kingdom's even children are put to death for stealing crumbs from a noble's table; whereas in ours we make every effort to feed those children, not take away their God-given right to life. And so, you men of transgressions are pent-up for a time to let you ponder your errant ways and hopefully become citizens under law. Speak not also of no honor in labor; for without labor there is no honor for mankind." He grabbed the rail of the quarterdeck and his eyes burned into the thief's; then they lighted on the other thieves who looked at the young prince with skepticism. He descended the steps and withdrew his sword. The crowd gasped, then shrieked as he raised the sword to the men tied together. With swift swoops his sword cut each man free. With gratitude and happy grins the thieves eyed the tall prince who turned a scowl to the defiant one and growled, "Speak not of oxen to me, though I will see to it that you shall finally work for a living." The defiant one folded under the authoritative grace of the young prince who he could see was meant to assert just and fair law.

The prince then softened as he scanned the many questioning faces, then his eyes lighted on the woman in tattered garb. "Fear not, good woman, for our goodly king has supplied us with ample provisions to last to our first happy harvest. Indeed, we are not sheep doomed to a barren land. Sheep and other livestock will come later after we till the soil with loving hoe and give it life. Aye, life with labor and love,…that is the promise. And speak not of food and shelter in church. The house of God is not a home. A home is in you, and we shall comb the island for wood, and thatch. Yea, together we shall bring out the hearth flaming in your dreams."

A little maiden leaning on a walking pole, hobbled out of the crowd and stood as straight as she could before the prince. She looked up with wide hazel eyes that seemed to glow all the more in contrast to her grimy face, which the prince could see that if washed, would be comely. Then she released one hand from her

93

pole and pressed it into his. "My good prince, I believe you. Truly, I wish for the honor of work. No one, it seems, thinks a cripple can work. 'Let them beg in the streets as long as it is not my street,' they say, or, 'What is the church for? Let the lazy sisters and monks take care of them.'" She released his hand and held hers up to him, then she let go the pole. Balancing herself on one leg she held up her other hand. "Though my legs are weak, these hands are strong." Then she toppled and the prince caught her in his arms. He carried her up the ladder and placed her in the captain's chair. She gave him an embarrassed look and pleaded, "Oh, prince, forgive me for being so clumsy, but do not treat me as being different. I've had enough of that all my life. Please place me among the rest of my people."

He glanced at her warmly as he pressed against the rail to face the people below. He said to her softly, "I too am part of the people." and then he smiled. "And you too are one of my people. Yet, take joy that we are each different, but not for the reason you think. For, you, girl, are different because of the hope against odds that is in your spirit." He looked down at them and said as he pointed to the girl, "Here, good people, is the living symbol of the promise. Aye, we shall inhabit the island of Promise and prove to our kingdom that all can lead useful lives — including a prince and this young girl on a walking stick — if those blest with good fortune would but perceive the worth in all humanity." The people cheered his words as the windlass turned and the sails ran up the mast.

The Knight And The Witch

T his was the age of chivalry when knights in shining armor went
on journeys to slay dragons and to protect the weak. One such
knight who was still very young was called before the king who
was very old and had no queen nor children. The knight bowed to
the king, then said, "My goodly king I am at your service."

The king nodded and said, "My good, Sir Youth, I know you have
not been a knight for very long and have not yet slain a dragon, yet
I have heard that you did save a little boy from the jaws of a wolf.
Because of this brave deed, I now award you with the honor of
searching the land for a new king."

The knight looked up showing surprise in his eyes. He said to the
king, "My lord, we have a king. What would we do with another?"
"True, but not forever am I to rule, you know....I am very old and
very tired. It is time to think about a new one," the king said with a
sigh."I feel I do not have much time left on earth"

"But my king, surely there are relatives, one of whom could take
your place when the king in heaven calls for you to help him rule."
"Alas, I have none. My poor, dear sister has left earth some five
years ago. And her dear daughter kidnaped long before."

"Then let me find the niece for you, my king,"the young knight
said excitedly."Why, when returned to you she will give you much
joy in your old age and then you will not talk of dying."

The old king rolled his eyes dreamily."Ah, yes, that would bring
untold joy. But, alas, much older and wiser knights years ago
searched the land and could not find her." He bowed his head and
rubbed his forehead and said sadly, "I fear she's dead."

"Then I shall find proof that she is, or return with your living
niece," the young knight said confidently.

95

"Ah, me, the expression of hopeful youth! But trouble not, my young knight," The king said with tears in his eyes; "I've already told you my most experienced and trusted knights could not. It is hopeless. Just go forth and fetch me someone who will rule the country." "There is always hope, your majesty — in old age as well," the knight reminded him, hoping to restore spirit in the king."And besides, who could be worthy enough to rule? How would I know? I know only one ruler. He can only be replaced by one of the same blood," the knight said kindly.

The king looked into the knight's eyes."That is no longer true. My ancestors long line ends with me. Go now and find a new line of kings."

"Then why not have one of your older and wiser errant-knights who are usually successful when in search of something for you?" "Aye, but aside from their search for my long lost niece, they simply go off to satisfy my greedy fancies. I have scores of chalices, magic weapons, and mystical scrolls to show for it. But now I want someone with a young and fresh insight to bring back a legislator to rival Moses."

"But, my lord, is that not just as fanciful? Where in this time and place can there be such another if not right in your own court?" "Bah, do not disillusion me with such trivial thinking — surely you can conceive of a ruler who will possess ideas to develop this nation to greatness which, I, alas, was never able to do. A king should be a sire who has in his dreams are of the future who would go beyond the skills of his father. Alas, with the untimely death of my young, devoted queen, I had no such aspirations."The young knight without hesitation said, "Aye, my lord, I now understand and that you are indeed, a king of vision rather than fancy." Then he could not look at his king directly and bowed his head."Excuse me, my king, but why is it you never remarried?"

The king searched for the knight's eyes and replied, "Such dreams spring from love, and I could not love another. And when my sister's dear daughter who was the apple of my eye, disappeared, so too did my hope for any kind of love." The king withdrew his sword and dubbed the knight's shoulder. "Go now, for in your youth, I see new hope."

The knight returned to his tent and prepared for his journey. He left his armor behind because there was no need. Slaying dragons or doing battle with murderers and thieves was not his purpose. He mounted his great black horse and rode out of the castle yard and across the moat bridge. That night he pulled up his horse at a little cottage in the middle of a dark forest.

He knocked on the door and an old woman with tangled gray hair answered it. He announced proudly, "I am a knight of the King's Advisory Table. I hope that you have enough food to feed me as I have traveled all day and am very hungry."

She cackled mixed with chuckles, "My, my, you seem too young to be a knight, much less to be giving advice to a king.... Could it be you are just a joking squire trying to deceive a gullible old lady as I am?"

He laughed and said good-naturedly, "Oh, good woman, young as I am, be assured I have been dubbed by my king because of noble deeds, not because of a youthful and wild imagination."

She looked into the handsome lad's innocent eyes, and could see that he was honorable. "Well, now," she said with a tight-lipped grin, "gullible or not, I see an honest lad, at least." The old woman sat him down at her kitchen table and said, "It is an honor to serve such a distinguished guest," she creaked and smiled, showing her gray gums as she had no teeth. "I am very poor so do not expect me to match the king's table."

97

He laughed, then said seriously, "Ah, but there is no matching your kindness." The old woman fussed over the cauldron, then, dragging her lame leg, turned revealing a small bowl of steaming stew. The knight thanked her, but hid his disappointment over the little bowl, for he was very hungry. As he was scraping the bowl with his spoon and hoping that the old woman would refill it, stew rose up to the brim. When the second stew was almost gone, again the stew rose up to the brim. Amazed, the young knight called to the old woman who was sitting by the hearth. "Old woman, how is it when I think the stew is finished, it replenishes itself?"

"Oh," she chuckled, "it doesn't do it itself. You see, how small the bowl is and I do not have any larger for a young man with a hearty appetite."

He looked at her puzzled. The knight scratched his head and said, "I think I see, but yet I don't."

She cackled with a grin on her wrinkled face, "You see, I have this lame leg."

"Yes, I see, for which I am very sorry. But what has that to do with the stew?"

"Well, because the bowl is so very small."

"Yes, I see, but what has that to with the stew magically reappearing before my eyes?"

She laughed and said, "Because I am lame." "Yes, I know," said the knight confused more than ever.

"Good, then you know I cannot keep getting up to serve you," she said, then sat back in her chair. "And I knew , of course, you wanted more."

"That's very generous of you," the knight said, smiling warmly. "But why not simply let me serve myself?"

"Oh, goodness, I couldn't do that — such a grand knight of the king's table."

The knight ate some more stew and reached the bottom of the bowl and again it grew to the top."Oh, my," he chuckled, "I shall grow too fat for my horse if I continue. Such magic I have never seen!" He pushed the bowl aside and said, "You must be a witch, but I never knew that witches could be so kind."

She leaned forward and slapped her good knee and said laughingly, "Oh, witches are like people — good and bad. And just like people they too have their ups and downs. I can be mean as well as kind." He got up from the table and walked over to the hearth to sit next to her. He could not resist looking in the pot. It was empty. He went back to the table to put the stew he had not touched into the pot because he felt guilty that he had eaten all her supper. But the bowl was empty and washed clean!

He returned to the hearth and sat down by her and said grimly, "I'm afraid I have eaten all your supper. I thought I had left a bowlful, but I suppose I ate that too."

"Oh, no, you didn't. I saw that you were finished so I washed the bowl," she said calmly.

"How could you I was sitting right there! You never hobbled over." He raised his brows.

"No, it's true. I told you my leg is weak. Still, I did wash the bowl."

"By Saint George, you are indeed a witch!" the knight yelped.

"It's true. But I've already told you I am," she chuckled.

He thought of the king's command and asked, "If you possess such magic, then perhaps you could help me. The king has sent me out to find a ruler, for his majesty fears he is near death's door."

She nodded a few times, then moaned, "Alas, it's true — soon the dread shall swing open." She looked at him gravely and ran her bony fingers through her tangled hair. "That is why I brought you

99

here."

His jaw dropped, and he inched to the edge of his chair. "You! Why, I came here of my own free will! — though I admit I was somewhat lost in the forest."

"You only thought you were lost because I willed you to the path to my home."

"Good grief, woman, why?"

She searched his eyes and asked, though she did not have to, "Did you not say you are on a quest for a ruler?"

He nodded, then shook his head in confusion. "Yes, but why lead me here?...Does this mean you will help me?"

"I don't have to — the quest is over." She giggled scratchily.

The knight put his hand on his hilt and snarled, "See here, witch, you are not thinking of spinning malice and holding me here under some spell!" He jumped up and drew his sword.

She crackled again. "My, my, you certainly have the temper of youth! No, my lad, sit down — have no fear. I'm still a kind old witch. But kind or not it is hard being a witch. Oh, our magic gives us many advantages; still, we have very little love in our hearts — most of us none at all...except..." her voice trailed off, along with a faraway look.

He slid his sword back in its scabbard and sat down. "Oh, but you seem to have softness in your heart," the knight said kindly.

"Ah, yes, I do — to a fault. So lonely was I many years ago that I did a dreadful thing. Yet I didn't care because it brought me happiness. Now — older, wiser and knowing the kingdom needs me — I am willing to give up that happiness."

The knight laughed heartily. "O witch you are not only a kind witch but a jolly jester as well! Why, I believe you are trying to tell me that you are the ruler for whom I search!" He rocked back on his chair and had an even heartier laugh.

She slapped her good knee, rocked back on her chair, too, and laughed but not as heartily. Then she leaned forward and waited for him to control his derisive guffawing. When he finally did and he sat up to face her again, she said to him gravely, "It is fortunate for you, young knight, that I am indeed a nice witch. Surely, you've heard what nasty witches do to those that mock them."

He snickered, "Oh, my, you wouldn't turn me into a frog, I hope." And he laughed again.

"Do not try my patience," she warned.

He coughed on his laughter and became wary as she stared coldly at him. "Truly, good and kind witch, I am sorry. But after all, you must admit the idea of your becoming our queen is silly."

"In your impetuous youth, you misunderstood. Of course, though a witch often interferes with human affairs, she has no use to control them—and surely not permanently," she explained in a soft, reasonable tone. "I simply meant that you must first know what a ruler is and then you shall have found royal command."

She raised herself up and limped to the hearth and took down a cup and a dipper. "Have some of this clear, hot barley brew and you shall understand." To his surprise, she dipped into the very same cauldron of stew that he has just seen bone dry and now she was pouring steaming hot barley broth into the cup. She handed it to the astonished young knight, who looked into her black mysterious eyes that reflected the flames flickering from the black sooty hearth. Then he felt the warmth of the cup in his hand and began to sip from it, hoping it would clear up the confusion in his head.

He looked up again and gulped his broth; he looked round the tiny cottage and she was nowhere in sight. Shaken by this he chugged down the broth and almost scalded his mouth. He looked all around for some cooling water. Then suddenly he felt the hot cup grow cold. He looked in and saw it was filled with cold water. Without wondering why, he drank it down to relieve his scorching mouth and hot throat. Relieved, he sat back a moment, anticipating that he would wake from a dream. Mysteriously the cup withdrew from his hand and floated to a dark corner where a bucket sat.

Suddenly puffed a light and tiny stars swirled as the light grew and lighted up the cottage corner. A delicate hand formed from one of the stars. It caught the cup and dunk it in the bucket. Then out of the whirling cloud shaped a lovely young maiden with long chestnut braids extended to her bodice. She stepped toward the knight with the cup in her hand and offered it to him. "Would you care for more water?...Or perhaps some more broth?...Or if you're still hungry, I can give you more stew," she said in a disarming voice that ran shivers down his spine. He took the cup from her hand without even knowing it as he popped his quizzical eyes at her blue orbs dazzling with confidence. "But you really should not stuff yourself so soon before you sleep; it can lead to awfully wild dreams." She giggled quaintly.

Still pop-eyed, he piped, "Aye, lovely lady, it seems I'm dreaming before I sleep."

She said laughingly, "Oh, yes, my tricky witch can make one think he's living out a dream. Though I assure you this is not a dream."

He cupped his face in his hands and wobbled his head, so flustered was he, and finally asked, "How can I be sure of that? In fact, how do I know you aren't a witch? — though lovely to be sure. Moreover, how do I know you are not the very same witch transformed?"

"Oh, she already told you about *me* — so how could I be myself and another?" she asked rhetorically but seriously.

He swept the red bangs on his forehead and tugged lightly on his red fuzzy chin, then said, "I cannot be sure of anything right now; yet I'm sure she did not mention you."

"Well, not directly." Her pixieish eyes brightened. She went to the tiny bed and propped up the pillow and drew down the coverlet. "You will see things more clearly after a good night's sleep."

"Oh, no," he yelped, shaking his head vigorously. "I shan't sleep for fear I shall dream some more. Besides, I am a knight of honor and surely not in the habit of stealing an old woman's bed."

"Oh, she's off to witches land. They never sleep in the kingdom," she said coolly.

"Oh, really? I never realized that...well, that is, I never used to have witches on my mind," he said with a snicker. "But all the more reason," he blushingly added while taking in her beauty, "that I should sleep outside under the trees and sky. For it seems, then, that this is your bed. Anyway, it's much too small for me. No, I shall rest outside beside my horse and start off early on my quest."

Her eyes glanced to the side, and she said, "Why, noble knight, I believe you are embarrassed — perhaps, a little frightened too that I might seduce you. Let it not worry you; I'll not turn you into a frog." She laughed.

"Then you heard? Why, you've been here all the while! You knew of the stew, though there was no stew." He jumped up and bent over the cauldron; it was empty. He looked back over to her. "And you knew of the barley broth, though there wasn't any of that either."

"Oh, is that so. Look again." She waved her hand mysteriously and the cauldron was piping with broth.

"I thought you said you weren't a witch?"

"Oh, but I'm not, I just learned a little about witchcraft during

103

my stay here."

"Stay?" he repeated. "You mean you're visiting?"

"I suppose, you could say that."

"Hmm, I've heard of such things....The witch is holding you captive, then?"

"At one time, perhaps that was so. And when she heard that my mother passed away, she begged me to forgive her and let me go. But what was there to go home to? My father had died years before, and my uncle always busy, so I decided to stay here. She is, after all, a very nice witch."

"Yes, so it seems. Still,..."

She broke in, "Oh, she really *is* and very intelligent. She has been my mentor all these years."

"Years?...How many years?"

"Oh, so many now I lost count....As I was saying, she's taught me much about the world and said someday whether I wanted to leave her or not, I should have to go into the world."

He looked at her with strange interest and asked, "What did she teach you?"

"Oh, just about everything there is to know," she said proudly.

He searched her bright intelligent eyes. "Such as?"

She lightly fingered her temple and said, "Oh, my, there's so much...." She pointed to the cauldron. "Well, did you know that the world is round?"

"Of course I know that — everyone but the lowest peasant knows it, though some do think it is square."

"Oh, you mean like a cube, a block?" she asked, trying to hide a smile.

"Of course, not. What would be the point of that? You would fall off the edge anyway!" he shook his head and chortled.

"Oh," she squeaked, "then you mean 'disk' when you say

round."

"Verily! What else?" He pounded his knee and laughed.

"A ball," she said seriously.

He guffawed mockingly. "Why that's as silly as a cube!"

"Not if the ball is spinning."

"Ridiculous, why we'd spin off into the sky!" He shook his head. "In truth, you are full of witches' tales!"

"Oh, really? Apparently you have never seen minstrels, then?

"Oh? And since when do they hold the wisdom of the ages?" he asked derisively.

"Are you telling me that you never saw them with great balance tread a wagon wheel?

"Of course, I've seen them do that? Even the peasantry has seen them do that — it is common knowledge. I have even seen them mount large rocks and make them spin."

Her brows rose and eyes sparkled. "Precisely, and they are so talented they don't fall, do they?"

He chuckled. "Not the skillful ones!...So?" He looked at her with a mixture of mild contempt and much humor.

"Well, the earth spins but because it is so huge we don't realize it," she said matter-of-factly.

He laughed uproariously. "Oh, my poor, sweet girl, you are bewitched! If the earth moved as such it would upset the movement of the stars, moon and especially the sun. Why, we could conceivably have day and night every three hours or as long as two, three days, depending on the direction and speed of its spin!"

It was her time to laugh. "It seems the schoolmen have bewitched you! The stars are fixed in heaven's night and the sun is a star. Only the planets circle the sun as they spin."

He arched his red brows in amazement because she spoke with

105

such apparent authority that he was beginning to believe her. He asked, "Then how do you explain that the sun comes up in the morning and then goes to bed in the evening?"

"The sun never sleeps. Ask the Chinese."

"What do they have to do with it?"

"Because they are on the other side of the world," she said insouciantly.

He ruffled his hair. "And the moon, too. I suppose, hangs its lamp on their otherside?"

She chuckled. "Where the earth goeth so doth the moon."

"Oh, my,…you are really serious, aren't you? Nor do you seem to be under a spell."

"Today's knowledge is under a spell!" she said definitively.

"Hm,…well, let's move to more practical knowledge." He stared into her bright eyes. "Tell me what else this witch of yours has taught you — let us say, politics, for instance."

Without hesitation she asked, "Did you know a king is not a king, really?"

He was disappointed in her. "Why, that's ridiculous. Of course a king is a king, the head of a kingdom."

She was disappointed in his response. "Naturally I did not imply he isn't called a king or that he is not the titular head of his kingdom. I meant that he does not rule over his people.…Of course, he does, but I suppose I'm saying that he shouldn't."

His curiosity piqued. Momentarily the knights' thoughts turned to his king's directive and wondered if there were some kind of mysterious connection. "Oh, and just what is a ruler, what does it really mean to rule?" he asked with expectations throbbing in his heart.

"Rules are disciplines that should come from the self, you know," she said as though he really understood. "Whereas a ruler is one who makes demands upon the kingdom."

The knight thought of the old woman's phrase and asked, "Isn't that the right of kings to make royal commands?"

She laughed. "Oh, my gracious, no!" Then she looked quizzically into his puzzled eyes and said, "Odd, you should use that term."

"Well, I just heard it from the old woman, but she didn't explain it."

She chuckled. "That's like her. She would rather you thought about it for a while. You see, there is no right to command. You must earn it. If you don't you are simply a ruler who makes demands on people who do not know why these demands are given. To command truly one must first be bestowed that right from the demands of the people. Once they have clearly expressed what these demands are in order to protect their interests and welfare, then the king commands that these demands not of his choosing are carried out. That my, good knight, is what a ruler is, for he then rules by royal command, which in reality means the people's commands." She was curious over his shocked expression. "Oh, my, noble knight, you had better lie down. You look so pale. Don't worry about me, I often sleep in the little stable out back. Yes, by all means, rest — you have a long journey ahead of you — a quest to keep, remember?"

"He stood up feeling faint, then regained himself and kneeled before her. He kissed her dainty hand and said, "No need for rest. My quest is done, my Queen."

107

The Princess and the Wishing Well

A distant kingdom long ago was without its king who had gone off with his knights to do battle against a warring tribe far to the north of this normally peaceful kingdom. A young beautiful princess missed her father and could not turn to her mother, the queen, who was in a coma from a mysterious illness. Tender care and affection bestowed on her by loyal servants of the castle were no substitute for the loving company of her parents.

One day as she was walking in her garden hoping for her father's return and her mother's speedy recovery, and taking in the wonderful fragrance of the many flowers in glorious bloom to pick for her mother, she first decided to test the superstition of the servants by heading for a well at the center of the inner ward of the castle. They had told her that the well had magical powers— that it was a wishing well for those only who had a true need for a wish to come true.

She leaned over the ledge and her golden tresses fell forward over her little shoulders. She looked down — her reflection clearly delineated in the pure water. Her bright blue eyes seemed to sparkle in the ripples of the spring's surging to the surface. She then jerked back and looked around to be sure none of the guards and workmen were looking at her. Her father had told her that such superstitions were only in the minds of the ignorant people and royalty should not harbor such nonsense.

Assured that no one was paying attention to her she leaned over again and said, "Oh, wishing well, if genuine you are, grant me my wish for surely there is no truer need." The spring's surge retired and the surface of the water became still. She saw her reflection fade, replaced by a wrinkled face of an old hag with fiery red eyes.

The princess blinked and turned her face away; never before had she seen such ugliness that put fear in her heart. So eager was the princess to have her wish granted, she nudged a glance back to the image in the water.

The hag grinned showing one yellow front tooth. The water began to bubble as she began in a gargling voice, "Truly I am what you say. I do grant wishes to those in need." Then she laughed hideously and almost choked from the water. She rose up so her mouth was above the surface. Her gargle turned to a gravelly echo as she said, "A pretty and beautifully dressed child as you surely can have no need."

"Oh, but I do; for what is a child without her mother?" the princess kindly protested.

"True, true, one should have a mother — I too had one, you know. I suppose it is hard for you to believe that I once was a child and a very beautiful one, I might add."

The princess admitted, "It's true, I should not think of a being as magical as you needing a mother, much less having one. But it is not as you suggest that I find it hard to believe that you were ever beautiful. For you see, my very own mother who was very beautiful, indeed, is now awfully deformed from her illness. I trust that if I were to spend my days in well water I too would soon wrinkle, and what beauty I may have be washed away."

The hag chuckled, and her frightening eyes once above the surface of the water gave way to a soft happy honey brown. "Well said, my child. No wonder you are destined to rule. Why, already you talk like a politician."

The quaint princess seemed surprised at first, then dismissed the remark with a chuckle. "Why do you speak of rule? My father reigns and surely if you grant me my wish, my mother will be well and bear him a son someday to become king some distant future when, alas, my father passes on."

The hag's scratchy voice echoed off the well's stones, "Aye, passes on, indeed....Enough of this....What is your wish?...Oh, yes, your mother, you say? But why waste a wish on her? Most want a wish for themselves."

"Oh," the princess was quick to reply, "it *is* for me — a daughter needs her mother. Nor can a daughter stand to see her mother suffer."

"Ah, but you say she is in a coma and therefore feels no pain," the old hag said, looking at the princess searchingly.

"Who can be sure of that? Besides, if not, I suffer for her," the princess answered with tears in her eyes. No longer were they bright but rather like a distant star: she thought of her poor mother wasting away; just then bells resonated in her ear. She turned to wipe away her tears when she saw a shaky figure venturing from the commons' outer ward, coming toward her.

She saw that it was a ragged boy, close to her own age, dragging himself along on a crude walking stick. As solemn bells grew louder. No sooner had she wiped away her tears when they flowed again for the boy, who was as pale as death. He tried to bow before her by sliding down on his pole. She quickly caught him and pleaded, "Oh, no, my darling boy, you are much too frail. Please do not try to bow before your princess. In your case, the attempt itself is more honorable than the deed."

"Perhaps for a princess near my age— but truly for a queen I should do the deed," he said with pride as he bowed his head.

"What's this you say?" Her eyes burned into his. He bowed his head; then braved another into her startled expression and bit his lip. "But surely you have heard, your majesty, and surely the bells. That is why I dared cross over to the inner ward to tell you how sorry

I am for your loss — ours,... the kingdom's loss."

She looked to the outer ward and saw women wailing and the parapet guards huddled in what appeared to be grim conversation. The keep servants behind her were skirting nervously and aimlessly in and out of the tower. Some were crying. Her eyes bulged with horror. She looked at the boy's eyes well up and said brokenly, "Before,...you addressed me as majesty, surely, you don't mean..."

"I fear I do, sweet queen. The village crier has announced throughout that the king died bravely in battle."

She nervously clutched the boy's collar and moaned, "Oh, no, no." The little boy touched her hand, took it in his grimy one and kissed the royal ring on her finger. "God bless you, my queen."

The distraught princess peered over to the hag shedding menace in her eyes, and ventured caustically. "You knew this all along, didn't you? How cruel of you to play witchery with me."

"Oh, not cruel, good *queen*, rather, I hoped to spare you for a while. Little did I know the news would travel from the north so fast," she said sadly and her eyes bore into the princess.

The little boy had thought the princess had gone mad because of the news he had blurted out until he leaned over and saw the face of the hag. "Then it's true!" he said, surprised. "This *is* a magic wishing well! But I had imagined a beautiful water maiden—never a wrinkled matron the likes of you!"

The hag grimaced, then laughed with good humor. "My sweet and bitter, bluntly perceptive boy, little do you grasp the finer meaning of what a great toll on one's constitution there is in granting wishes."

The princess said harshly, "Humph, what wish have you granted? Surely, you could have inferred that I would have wished my father safe."

"Oh?" the hag perked, "At the expense of your mother?"

The young queen stepped away and wrung her hands, then turned back to the well. "Such a cruel, callous question!" She leaned over further and squealed, "And must you stay down in this silly well? Would that you come up out of there so we can talk like civil beings."

"As you wish — after all, you are my queen."

"Do not mock me; nor do I wish to waste my wish on you."

"I'm afraid you already have," the witch chuckled and pulled herself up by the winch-rope. She shook out her soaked cloak and with each heel of her hands she tapped water from her large ears. She then proceeded to wring out her long straggly hair that resembled seaweed.

"What! Are you saying because I wished you here out of the water that I can no longer wish my mother well?"

"No, I didn't say that. Truly, you are free to wish her well."

"Again you play words with me," the princess said bitterly: "Don't forget, the wish is to be granted only if there is a need."

The hag shook more water from her hair and noted, "Oh, truly, there was a need. I'm afraid another hour in that well would have been the end of me. It's devilishly cold down there, you know."

"That is of no concern to me," the princess snapped.

"Oh, but it is; for you are queen now and must concern yourself with your subjects," she reminded her as she motioned her bony hand toward the boy.

"That I'll not deny; but that does not concern you — surely, you are no subject of mine."

"Oh, but it does concern me," the hag responded sharply. "You see I am very old and incapable of the ordeal of this act in the well. Why, it might be years before I could repeat this fatiguing rôle." She placed her hand on the boy. "This dear boy shall have died in the meantime."

The boy recoiled from her and shouted, "Don't believe her, your majesty. She's a witch for sure and is trying to lay more grief upon you. Though I am a cripple, I am strong in spirit and do not intend to die until I'm as old as she."

The old hag looked down at the boy with curious kindness in her soft brown eyes, the whites of which returned, having lost the sting of well water. "Hush, dear boy, you know not of these matters. Better that you don't, but now that I have said it — your legs are but a symptom of a more serious illness that will travel to your heart."

"Fie on you!" cried the princess. "To utter such horror before the dear boy is unforgivable." The princess hugged the boy and said, "Heed not the hag — you are right: she is a wicked witch." She then braced herself and looked at the hag coldly and squarely in the eyes. But to her surprise she observed a saintly expression in the hag's face. The princess gasped, "My God, you speak the truth — you do see dreaded death lurking in the forces of things to come!" She fell to her knees and buried her face in the old hag's soaked cloak. "Oh, sweet woman, you must do something for the boy. You said he shall have died, and not simply and cruelly that he shall, but that he *must die*; then surely he shall have lived if you act now."

"Oh, but you've spent yourself. You wished me from the well, remember?" She laughed hideously and her kind look dissolved, giving way to meanness.

The princess stood up and crossed her arms in regal fashion and said, "Oh, no, I saw your true look before. You are toying with me again. No one in the wide-world could be this cruel! If indeed I am

113

now queen — and this is not some other callous trick — would you expect me to rule with such a horrid attitude that I not kindly trust my subjects? Is that not the excuse for monstrous tyrants?"

"My, my, you *do* have royal talent!" the witch said, arching her unkempt brows. However, I *do* have honor, and I admit I tricked you; therefore you may wish me back."

"But what good would that do me…and this dear lad?" the princess asked, squinting at her.

The witch pondered, "Well, that would then make it even, and entitle you to wish to have your mother well — that is, unless you want your father back alive." Her now clear eyes brightened from the prospect of such a decision.

"Fie, that's ghoulish — why, the devil himself would not strut before me the horns of such dilemma!" the princess howled, clutching at the hag's cloak.

"Of course, there is always the strong probability that I'll not have the strength after that to grant a wish to the boy," she speculated, rubbing her narrow pointed chin.

The princess stood up and paced round the well. "Is there never soft resting places in the twining of your ordeals?" she asked as she threw up her arms to the sky.

"You will soon learn as *queen* that life consists of hard choices," the hag lectured.

The princess paused, fingered her tresses and asked, facing the hag, "How do I know what you say is true — that this darling boy is soon to die?"

"You don't; neither do you know I can restore your father's life, or your mother's health," the hag said cryptically jutting out her chin and searching the princess' lackluster eyes, which seemed to have sunk into her head.

"Please, my queen, don't listen to her!" the boy begged sliding down his walking stick to bow before his queen but he fell down and gnarled in pain and clutched his heart. He lifted his face from the ground and screeched, "She is a nasty old witch who enjoys torturing innocence!"

The hag shook her head and said with genuine sadness, "No, my boy, if only it were a cruel game — soon you would get over it."

The queen kneeled before the boy who was panting and struggling to lift himself up on his stick. She kissed him on his grimy cheek and lifted him to lean upon his stick. Then glancing up at the hag, she commanded, "Cure him immediately. I want him to rise up without the use of his stick. If you do not grant this wish and make him whole, I swear I shall toss you back into the well myself."

The hag scratched out a hearty laugh and looked upon the princess with skepticism. "You would do this for this ragged lad at the expense of your mother?"

The princess turned away from them, paced and looked up at the castle window of her mother's room. She turned back to them. She looked softly at the lad and smiled. Then sternly she looked into the witch's eyes and said, "Well, what are you waiting for? Cure my darling subject."

"Oh, no, my queen, please, let me die nobly for the queen mother!"

"Hush, lad," said the queen. "You have a long promising life ahead of you. I trust you will serve the crown and country well."

The boy wrestled with his walking stick to bow before her. "Oh, my belovéd queen, if healthy, I swear before you I shall be your champion."

She reached out to steady his hand and to check him from bowing. "Good, then you can begin now by not painfully kneeling

115

before me." She glanced over at the witch. "Cure him instantly, I say."

Never before did this witch hear such a tone of command spoken to her. She eagerly bent over the boy, placing her hand on his pate. He recoiled and dropped to his knees with pain and rolled away on his back and begged, "Oh, no, my queen, forgive me, but I cannot let you!...You must not do this for me. Think first of your mother, ...your father the king!"

The hag glanced up. The princess nodded without hesitation and firmly ordered, "Do it now, I say!"

The hag mumbled under her breath as she held down the resistant lad. There was a glow about her hand. It diffused to her hair. The princess could see streaks of shiny chestnut midst the seaweed look. Then the witch stood up and raised her glowing hand above him and ordered him to rise. He reached for his stick, but she kicked it away. "Unassisted you are to rise."

The boy bounced up miraculously; he looked down at his legs, then felt them. He chuckled and with a broad grin he looked at the queen. He touched his legs again. "Oh, my queen, my legs have life in them!" He danced round her, then bowed before her and kissed her hand repeatedly. "Oh, to be blest with such a queen!"

"And what of me?" the old hag said with some disappointment.

The boy guffawed, "Oh, yes, yes, to be blest with such a loathsome witch — who yet does kind things! But nothing do you do for my lovely queen and therefore you are loathsome still."

"Hush, good subject," the queen cautioned with a smile. "Just seeing you before me — so strong and straight upon your legs is the fulfillment of my wish."

The hag lightly and playfully paddled the boy on his rump and snickered, "Still, think me a witch, eh?...Perplexed you are that with good comes bad, eh?" She popped her lips and grinned.

"Well,... maybe some good...when gallantry from an unexpected source proves her mettle as does your little queen." She glanced at the princess who for a moment had turned to her mother's window. "Are you having regrets, dear queen?" the witch asked with a curious squint in her eyes.

"Not at all! My mother and father brought me up right. The subjects of the realm come first. There can be no question. So, you see, there never was any other choice to make."

"Then why do you keep looking up at the window?" The witch asked. "Surely your mother isn't there."

She smiled kindly at the witch, "I know, I just hope she can forgive me for my stern justice."

"Oh, and why shouldn't she?...After all, it is the very thing that has saved her." she looked softly at the young queen.

The hag's face seemed less shriveled and much kinder to the queen who thought she saw tears running down her cheek while finally asking her, "My sweet witch, what is it you mean?"

The witch smiled and spun herself round rapidly several times, and the boy and princess stared wide-eyed at the blurred layers of transformation with each turn. When she stopped and faced them, in her stead was the queen mother in all her healthful beauty. She swept away the chestnut hair from her honey eyes and stared at them as though she had just woken from sleep, indeed, from her coma.

The princess jumped and squealed with joy as she rushed to hug her mother tightly, lest she slip away like a dream. She then stood back to inspect her cloak and saw that it was her mother's regal robe. She touched her mother's long shiny chestnut hair and felt it dry.

"What is all the fuss about?" the mother asked. "And what am I

117

doing out here in the ward? Let us walk awhile among the flowers, then gather them to brighten the keep's chambers. Hopefully my monarch will be home soon."

In her happiness that all was not lost, and in the end her true choice of the heart had come true, the princess delayed telling her mother of the king's death. She guided her still frail mother to the garden, then looked over at the boy and then the well, and muttered, "Yes, the monarch is home." Her bright blue eyes were restored, but for a fusion of tears for the king.

Tower of the Millennium

While great earth turned from the tenth century to meet the sun's celebration of a new century, a slip of a girl stirred in her little, comfortable bed. Early dawn's rosy rays pierced the tower window of the cylindrical chamber, then diffused through a sheer bed curtain, shedding its pink calling upon the velvet surface of the bed. The girl opened her sleepy eyes, sat up, stretched, yawned and threw off mounds of heavy furs. Withdrawing from under her pillow an old book, she fondly tapped it, then slid it back. She swept back the curtain. Bounding out of the bed she ran across the cold flag stones to the tiny window. She leaned to the brisk, cold air and looked through the slowly dispersing morning mist down upon the castle courtyard. Stirring only were a cat still stalking creatures of the night in the early morning shadows and a monk solemnly pacing while murmuring morning prayers. She rested her elbows on the window's ledge and cupped her dawn-rose cheeks with her palms.

Now wide from expectation of a new century, her eyes cast rich purple toward the sun's shy peep round the mountain side. She forced a faint smile and sighed, "Hello, year 1000, I do hope you will usher in purpose for me." Then she bent her eyes to the west and high in the sky she waved to the paling moon of the last century and said cheerfully, "And goodbye to you, 999."

A rooster crowed and chickens cackled. She looked down again at the courtyard, surprised that the customary heavy clouds did not wrap the tower. Its dark grey had turned pink when dawn jumped the castle wall. A busy flock was pecking at the icy skin of muddy cartwheel ruts. One by one tradesmen, marketers, wash-women and water-maidens began their day's work with unusual gusto. Icy winds brushed by. She shivered and crossed her arms and ducked back in. Tossing a frayed robe over her shoulders, she sat on the edge of the bed. The girl drew up her blue-white feet and rubbed away the cold, then stretched the robe to cover them. Resting her quaint chin on her drawn up knees she sighed, "Oh, I wish I had a friend — why the tower is so high in the clouds nary a bug, nor bird, not even a mouse comes up for me to talk to." She tugged on her tangled black curls draping her cheeks and dried her trickling tears.

Just then a powdery green glow filled the tiny window, then wafted across the flagstone floor and danced in front of her. Startled, the darkhaired girl drew back and tossed the heavy bed furs over her head. Hearing a muffled toot of a horn she peeled back the furs to peek. Hopping on what looked like bent sticks the legs of the

119

luminous outline carried its round pillowy body about the room. All in green and tooting a little horn was a round little man with a cherubic face despite his age. His cheeks puffed red over a fuzzy white beard while he huffed and puffed on his little tin horn, the sound of which faintly bounced off the chamber's concave wall.

She relaxed, then slid to the edge of the bed. She giggled at the sight. The little man looked up at her with great round eyes as clear as diamonds, then he began to jig and waved her on as though she should dance too. She joined in and skipped around the tiny room as his tin ear toots grew to a resonant, fluid tune. Though the girl had never danced, her clumsy skips soon refined to graceful steps and began twirling round the room like the maidens of the wards below whom she would observe through the clouds during festivals. She laughed too, like she had never laughed before. The cruel fact was she never had, except when a bluebird perched on her window sill so long ago that she forgot that it had sung to her:

> Dark princess of the
> tower Gloomy be no more;
> Dawn will shower
> Thee with power
> To swing out the door.

Exhausted, she threw herself back on the bed. She gasped for breath. Feeling faint from the cold chilling her perspiration, she drew up the covers. The little man in green hopped up on the chest at the foot of the bed to catch his breath. She stared in wonderment at her visitor as she regained her breath and felt her blood flowing warmly. She was certain that she had never felt better. She smiled at him, searching his great round eyes, and asked, "Who are you?"

"Why, the new year, of course," he said rather bluntly, then proudly added, playing with the drawstring of his green kirtle, "Actually more important than that, I am the millennium." And he puffed a burst into his horn.

Looking at him with amused curiosity, she asked, "Forgive me, gentle one, but why are you old if you are indeed the new year?"

He removed his floppy hat and scratched his bald ruddy head and said, "Oh, but they are never entirely new."

"Oh, but verily this one must be!" she said more hopefully than convincingly.

"Why, yea, considering it marks a thousand of them...Hm, I wonder why they didn't think of swaddling clothes — aye, how fitting that would be!...Oh, well,..."

"But why come here — to me?" she asked with strained confusion. "Where else, who else?...After all, are we not of the same cut?"

Her eyes now flashed blue from the later light of morning. "We are?... My, do I resemble you?— though surely I am taller. I have tried many times to see my reflection. After they hand the tin plate of food through the bolted door and I have eaten, I would polish the tin-plate and take it to the window's light, but never did I appear!"

"That seems to me to make sense....But oh, goodness, I don't mean that you look like me — simply the 'ness' of it! Why, you're a bonny princess and I'm just a plain, ugly elf." He smiled, reached over and touched her face. "I see you cannot see yourself....Do you know you have a smudge on your face?" Then he lightly tugged her hair. "And your hair — such beautiful raven hair — is untidy."

She flushed with embarrassment, then dampened her fingertips with her tongue and rubbed her face clean. She tossed back her hair and tried to brush it with her hand. She pondered the word — the bluebird came back to her.

"Oh, much better," he observed with a chuckle. He took out a little handkerchief. "But you missed." Reaching over he rubbed her

121

upper cheek. He stretched behind him and pulled out of nothingness a comb of pearl and handed it to her.

Her eyes danced with excitement while she luxuriated in the combing of her hair until she struggled with the tangles and became frustrated. "Oh, what difference does it make?" she moaned and put down the comb. "No one sees me; I see no one — except till now." "Ah, yes, till now." he said wistfully.

"I do not mean to be rude, little man; but I trust you do not really care how I look."

"Aye, that's true; yet appearances do mean something in this world and you must be ready."

"Ready for what — my next meal? Good grief I see nothing but a grubby hand poised through the door waiting for me to receive my cup and plate."

"Oh, there will be no more of that. I meant you must be ready for the new year."

"So?" She scratched her head. "The new year is here — ready for what — the next new year?"

"You'll see," he said with a toothless, elfish smile.

She picked up the comb again and fighting the tangles, she asked, "What did you mean when you said we were of the same cut?"

He did not have to ponder and said confidently, "We are of the new millennium."

"How mysterious! And just what is that supposed to mean?" she queried impatiently.

"That we have no contact with the dark past," he said calmly. She put down the comb and leaned over with a curious glint in her eyes. "Are you saying you were just born?"

"Just as you are. In a sense, yes, though obviously I, too, am full grown," he said innocently.

122

She laughed heartily to his wide-eyed surprise. Then she cupped her dainty hand over her mouth and convulsed. Stiff-lipped she said, "Forgive me for laughing. It — 'full grown' — just struck me funny, coming from an elf." She slid to the foot of the bed to lean forward. She pecked him on the forehead. Then she sat back and said, "But how does that make us in common? I was born in the last century — how, then like you could I have been just born? I estimated that the year was 984."

"Very good — you're close. But how does that make us different? Of course, you had a wet-nurse with you in your infancy and a maiden to look after you in your early years. Nevertheless, you've been locked in and for the most part alone."

"Alas, 'tis true…very alone…like living inside that trunk you're sitting on.…And it seems forevermore I shall be sealed within this towering tomb," she said heavily. She gathered one side of her long hair, tossing it forward over her breast, and she picked up the comb again.

"My, you are a gloomy wench — in truth, too long in the clouds," he chuckled. "How happy you were dancing before. You should retain that vigor and exciting attitude; for there is much for you to do."

She tugged her tangles with the comb and rasped with sarcasm, "Oh, yes, by all means — there's much more dying I must do, I suppose."

"Shush, my child, speak not of dying when you haven't really been born yet," he cautioned.

"Oh, that it were so!" she cried. "Yet, I suppose, in a way it's true, depending how one looks upon it. Either way, I haven't lived. In order to die, I trust one should first have had a mother and father." She retrieved her book from under the pillow and absently

123

leafed through the worn pages.

"Oh, everybody has had a mother and father — even elves," he assured her as he eyed 𝔓lato in cloister black lettering on the cover.

"I hadn't. You said yourself: I haven't been born."

He removed his hat and scratched his bald head. "Well, I meant, that you have and you haven't. That is Time made a mistake and deposited you in the wrong slot, so to speak."

"Oh?" she remotely perked, lightly, absently stroking her hair with the comb.

"Yes,. . .sort of an accident, you might say."

She snapped out of it and dropped her comb. "Is that all I am — an accident? Yes, I suppose, that is what I am. I always felt as though I was some kind of unwanted intrusion."

"Oh, perhaps, but not unwanted."

"How can an accident or an intrusion be anything but. . ."

"Oh, but this accident will work out splendidly. Now, they don't have to wait for you to grow up. . . .Yeah, capital is the mystery of fate!" He put his finger to his lips. "Shush,. . .listen. . . .Do you hear the bells?"

She bent an ear. "Why, yes, I do. . . .It's tolling the new year. I recall their doing that in other years. Yet the sound is different."

"Not happy?" he queried.

"Why, yes,. . .they sound. . .well, rather sad."

"Aye, well it should be. The king is dead." "The king?" "Aye, your father."

"What!" she rasped. "I have no father, that is, I don't think I do. . . .Good grief! Is that why you called me princess?"

"Aye."

"But how can this be! What father — and a king to boot — would imprison his own daughter?"

124

"Accident, remember? Your time is now."

"Time? Time for what?" She was wringing her hands now.

He snapped, "To rule."

"Why, that's ridiculous. How could I rule — I know nothing."
She picked up her comb. "Is my hair looking better to you?"

"Perfect,...regal."

She giggled. "Oh, you are a mischievous, taunting little elf!"

"You think me thus because you are confusing ignorance with
innocence," he said soberly. "Aye, the more I think on it — it was
no accident, no mistake, though but a shadow in a cave. They
knew,...of course," he added, pointing to the book, "you had your
friend all these years"

"They?" she perked.

"Yes, the vital forces — knew exactly what they were doing —
nurturing you to the right age, yet maintaining your innocence,
unscarred by the darkness of an age. Aye, how fitting! A brand new
millennium ushered in by a freshness — yea, yea, a soft but
compelling breeze to sweep away the odorous staleness from a
thousand years in the dark."

She stared perplexedly at the window now flooded with bright
sunlight. The bluebird lighted on the sill and re-chirped its song
from so long ago.

She jumped out of the bed and ran to the heavy door. She
pressed against the door; oddly, she was not surprised that it was
unbolted. When she opened it all the way, a flood of green light
rushed before her from spiral steps below. She reeled on her heels;
she noted her feet were not cold. The room was gone; only the edge
of darkness faced her. She swung back to the steps, blinking her
eyes at the light.

A myriad of faces focused along the steps. Their lips moved,

125

chanting: "God save the Queen! God bless our Queen Lux."

Her eyes brightened and she radiated a smile — she understood. "Yea, my people, out from the shadow I am the light to lead you through this green, hopeful mist of unchartered time to the second millennium whereupon ideas will shrug off its dark cloak and glow with beneficial meaning from here into the next thousand years."

Sparta Reborn

Once upon a time there was a king who ruled over a vast wasteland. His subjects naturally were very poor because of the lack of the kingdom's resources. Year after year they tilled the soil to feed the king's court, the army and themselves barely. During the winter months to stay alive the poor subjects had emigrated to a neighboring land called Goshen as it was a land of plenty to work its mills and handcraft shops.

The officials of Goshen welcomed the people of Wasteland because their own people had grown fat and content from their fortunate heritage. This expedient relationship went on for many years. Goshenians grew fatter and Wastelanders thinner. The more wealth the migrant workers returned with, the more the cruel king of Wasteland exacted. As a result the king became more prosperous and powerful and lavished festivities upon his court. The Army too was rewarded—if it exhibited excellence in war skills training.

Some of the bolder emigrants, disillusioned by the cruelty of their own country, remained in Goshen, slipping off to rich farm lands where the land gentry were eager to employ such dedicated workers. Eventually entire families deserted Wasteland to the chagrin of tax-collectors.

Goshen was delighted with these turn of events; for after a decade not one Goshen citizen was engaged in menial tasks. But its army too had become indolent and too well-fed.

The population of Wasteland dwindled drastically, the court pleaded with the king to take action. The king did nothing. Eminent nobles of the court sent dispatches to the commandant of Wasteland's army. Always they were returned with the seal unbroken. There was not one among the court who could face the crisis since all were strangers to ordeal. They roamed about the luxurious court and gardens sniveling to their ladies about the cowardice of the king and bemoaning the diminishing coffers that would inevitably lead to their impoverishment. Still, they continued their lavish ways.

In contrast, the king had turned to an ascetic life, never partaking the court festivities and remaining in his chambers in reclusion. The few times he did take the throne for matters of state, the court was astonished by his gaunt appearance. On occasion he would visit the army camp to assist the officers in keeping morale high during incessantly rigorous training with meager reward.

A decade had passed, and now even the nobility was fleeing the country for a better life at Goshen whose own nobility sympathized with them and readily accepted them because of their noble birth. One evening a special detachment of the palace guards on horseback thundered across the drawbridge after months of touring the kingdom. The officer in charge with scroll in hand dismounted

127

in the inner ward and headed for the king's keep.

The officer was astonished upon entering the outer chambers by the bleak, Spartan ambience. All furnishings and art work had been removed; the king's magnificent desk table of marble and mahogany had been replaced by a peasant's table and the chopped remains of the throne were by the fireplace, which barely glowed. When he entered the king's sleeping quarters, he was even more taken a back: the great bed was gone and in its place was a thin layer of straw and an old horse-blanket upon which the king was kneeling in prayer. The officer waited until the king stood up and greeted him: "Welcome, captain, to my humble quarters ... .Now, what have you to report after so long a journey?"

The captain cleared his throat and overcame his shock over the king's bowed, emaciated appearance. "Your majesty, the mission is accomplished." He handed the king the scroll.

The king waved it off. "My eyes are not what they used to be. Please, captain, read it to me." The captain unrolled it and strained his eyes in the dim light. He shook his head and rolled up the scroll again. "I shall simply tell you about it, good king....All the villages and towns have been scoured and all the people but the sick and agéd have vanished."

The king mustered a smile and said, elatedly, "How marvelous!...Yet sad that the few have been abandoned. I trust you rewarded them for staying?"

"Oh, yea, your majesty, as you ordered."

"Good, they deserve it, poor souls. That is my one regret." The king tugged absently on his whiskers. "And the grain bins?"

"Thoroughly diminished, but for a few bushels here and there that I had to use as provisions for my men."

"Excellent! And the noblemen consigned to your charge? How fare they?"

"Out of the forty-five of your courtiers only six remain as true soldiers of the king."

"Oh?...And I take it the others deserted?"

"Nay, my liege, only a few made the attempt for which they were executed. The rest simply died from exhaustion or exposure. Three died nobly in the saddle."

"But six survived, eh?—miraculous!...Perhaps, in time they might warrant a commission of leadership."

"I shouldn't doubt it, my king; they are proven noblemen."

The king stroked his whiskers and asked, "And what of their ladies, what was their reaction to my dictum?"

"As you directed we left a contingency at each district of mercy, only a few protested, most women seemed relieved that they were chosen to be useful."

"I'm happy to hear that—motivation is important. According to the Mother Superior's report they have taken admirably to nursing the sick and tilling the nunnery gardens." The king went to a dark corner and retrieved a suit of armor. "It appears, then, we are ready." He handed the captain sealed orders. "Take this to the commandant. This is one order he will open." The king laughed.

Thence in a few weeks, Goshen fell to the Spartan trained soldiers of Wasteland.

Author's Wishful Thinking

Whimsical perhaps is earnest leaning
toward the sad and merry tales of yore
lending far-off yet relevant meaning
by simply merging with fantastic lore;
thereby suspending modern frauds —
like the excess yen for iPods.

Other works by author:

*A Tale of Love & War [Saga of The Great Depression, WWII home
front and action in the Pacific]*

Modest Impressions [small book of poems]

Angel Queen [Medieval fantasy of epic proportions]

*In Defense of Eve [Medieval clash of two immortals, and
knights]*

Politics: Then & Now [Criticism of modern politics]

*Drama Collection: One & Three Act Plays [Designed for high
school classes and drama clubs]*

Philosophic Presumptions [Journeyman's effort]

*Sundry Short Stories [written over years concerning the human
condition.*

*All selections displayed on Lulu & other Internet
bookstores as paper backs and eBooks*

Author and
Wife enjoying a
night out long ago

Author's Grandchildren

www.ingramcontent.com/pod-product-compliance
Lightning Source LLC
Chambersburg PA
CBHW031608260626
47154CB00020B/1709